BORZOI
BOOKS

FIFTY
YEARS

ALSO BY *Friedrich Duerrenmatt*

TRAPS (1960)

THE PLEDGE (1959)

These are BORZOI BOOKS, *published in New York*
by ALFRED · A · KNOPF

Once a Greek . . .

Once a Greek...

BY

Friedrich Duerrenmatt

ac. Dürrenmatt

Translated from the German by

RICHARD AND CLARA WINSTON

New York: Alfred · A · Knopf

1 9 6 5

L. C. catalog card number: 65–11110

THIS IS A BORZOI BOOK,
PUBLISHED BY ALFRED A. KNOPF, INC.

Published June 14, 1965
Third Printing, July 1965

Originally published as *Grieche Sucht Griechin.*
Copyright 1955 by Peter Schifferli, Verlags AG.
"Die Arche," Zurich

Once a Greek . . .

It had been raining all day,

all night, for weeks. The streets, the avenues, the boulevards, gleamed with wetness. Rivulets, brooks, little streams, flowed along the curbs. Automobiles splashed through water; people walked under umbrellas, shrouded in raincoats, their shoes soggy, their socks permanently damp. The atlantes, putti, and caryatids that supported the balconies of mansions and hotels, the sculptures that clung to the façades, trickled and dripped; thin streams of water ran down them, dissolving the bird droppings; and the pigeons sought shelter under the Greek gables of the Chamber of Deputies and between the legs and breasts of patriotic statuary. It was a miserable January. Then came the fog, and it too went on for days and weeks. It was accompanied by an epidemic of grippe, not especially dangerous for respectable people of substance, but it did carry off a few old uncles and aunts, to the delight of their heirs, as well as several venerable statesmen. Otherwise the only victims were the clochards who slept under the bridges by the river. And the fogs were succeeded by more rain. And still more.

His name was Arnolph Archilochos, and Madame Bieler behind her counter would say: "The poor boy. Such an impossible name. Auguste, bring him another glass of milk." And on Sundays she said: "Bring him another Perrier."

She addressed her husband, thin as a rail, winner of a legendary Tour de Suisse and runner-up in an even more legendary Tour de France, who served his customers in his cyclist's getup, a yellow jersey. (His café was the center for a small group of cycling fans.) But Auguste did not agree. "Georgette," he would say in the morning when he got up, or in bed, or behind the stove after everyone had left and he could warm his thin, hairy legs, "I don't understand your fondness for Monsieur Archilochos. He's not a man, he's all bottled up. A fellow can't go on drinking nothing but milk and mineral water all his life!"

"That's all you drank once upon a time," Georgette replied in her deep voice, placing her arms akimbo, or, if she were in bed, folding them over her mountainous bosom.

"I grant it," Auguste Bieler admitted after long reflection, during which he vigorously massaged his legs. "But that was when I was training for the Tour de Suisse, and I won it in spite of those high passes, and nearly won the Tour de France too. When it's something like that, abstinence has some point to it. But for Monsieur Archilochos? Why, he's never even slept with a woman. And the man is forty-five."

This matter also bothered Madame Bieler, and she always became embarrassed when Auguste began to speak of it, whether in bed or fully clothed in his cyclist's getup. As a matter of fact, there was no denying that Monsieur Arnolph, as she called Archilochos, had certain principles. For example, he did not smoke either. Swearing was even more out of character. Moreover, Georgette could not even imagine him in a nightshirt, let alone naked—so correct was his manner, so completely dressed the impression he made, although he also seemed very poor.

His world was fixed, punctual, ethical, hierarchic. At the top, at the summit of his world order, his ethical cosmos, the President of the country sat enthroned.

"Believe me, Madame Bieler," Archilochos would say, gazing reverently at the portrait of the President in its carved frame, which hung above the orderly array of brandy and liqueur bottles behind the counter, "believe me, our President is a sober man, a philosopher, almost a saint. He does not smoke, does not drink, has been a widower for thirty years, has no children. You can read it in the newspapers."

Madame Bieler did not dare to take issue with this directly. She, too, like everyone in the country, had some respect for the President. He was, after all, the only fixed point in the passing parade of governments. On the other hand, such a paragon made her nervous. She preferred not to believe it.

"You say it's in the newspapers," Georgette therefore replied hesitantly. "All right. But who knows what the real truth is? Everyone says the newspapers are full of lies."

That was a common fallacy, Archilochos replied; at bottom the world was ethical. Solemnly, deliberately, he sipped his Perrier as if it were champagne, and added: "Auguste also believes the newspapers."

"No," Georgette said. "I know better. Auguste doesn't believe a word he reads in the newspapers."

"Why, doesn't he believe the scores on the sports pages?"

Madame Bieler could think of no reply to that.

"Virtue is something apparent," Archilochos continued, cleaning his rimless, slightly crooked glasses. "It shines in this face, as it shines in the face of my Bishop."

Whereupon he turned toward the portrait that hung over the door.

"The Bishop is a little too fat," Madame Bieler protested. "He can't be all that virtuous."

Archilochos' faith was unshakable.

"That is his nature," he replied. "If he did not live virtuously, philosophically, he would be even fatter. Now look at Fahrcks, on the other hand. How excitable, how intemperate, how arrogant. Sinful in every respect. And conceited."

He jerked his thumb over his right shoulder at the portrait of the notorious revolutionary.

Madame Bieler stuck to her guns. "You certainly can't call him conceited," she declared. "Not with that snout and that mop of hair. And with his love of the masses."

7

"That is only a particular kind of conceit," Arnolph maintained. "I can't see why you have that demagogue's picture hanging here. Why, he's just come out of jail."

"Oh, you can never tell," Madame Bieler replied, downing a whole glass of Campari. "You can never tell. You have to be careful in politics."

The Bishop—let us turn back to him; the portrait of Fahrcks hung on the opposite wall—the Bishop was Number Two in Monsieur Archilochos' hierarchic world. He was not a Catholic bishop, although Madame Bieler was a good Catholic after her fashion, who went to church—when she went—in order to weep fervently (but she wept just as fervently at the movies). Nor was he a Protestant bishop. Auguste Bieler, an immigrant from German Switzerland, "the fastest thing on two wheels Switzerland has produced" (*Sports,* 9/9/29), could not possibly recognize any but a Zwinglian bishop (though also after his own fashion; he had no idea that he was a Zwinglian). No, the Bishop was head of the Old New Presbyterians of the Penultimate Christians, a somewhat peculiar and amorphous sect imported from America. He was hanging over the door only because Archilochos had entered the bar, portrait under his arm, and introduced himself to Georgette.

8

That had been nine months ago. In May. When there were great splashes of sunshine on the street outside, slanting rays of sunlight inside, Auguste's yellow jersey and his sad cyclist's legs, under a hazy shimmer of hair, shining like molten gold.

"Madame," Archilochos had said timidly, "I am here because I notice the portrait of our President in your restaurant. Hanging over the counter, in a prominent place. As a patriot, I am reassured. I am seeking a place in which to take my meals. A home. But I must always have the same table, preferably in a corner. I am alone, a bookkeeper, live righteously, and am a strict teetotaler. I do not smoke either. Bad language is also against my principles."

Then they had settled on a price.

"Madame," he had then said, handing her the portrait and looking at her woefully through his small, smudged glasses, "may I ask you to hang this Bishop of the Old New Presbyterians of the Penultimate Christians. Preferably next to the President. I can no longer eat in a room where he is not present. That is why I have just left the Salvation Army restaurant, where I used to have my meals. I revere my Bishop. He is an example to us all, an absolutely sober, Christian person."

And so Georgette hung up the picture of the Bishop

of the Penultimate Christians, though only over the door, where he remained mum and content, a man of honor, although sometimes denied twice and thrice by Auguste. For if people happened to ask who the old gent was, Auguste used to answer: "A patron of cycling."

Three weeks later Archilochos appeared with another picture. This time it was a photo, autographed, of Petit-Paysan, owner of the Petit-Paysan Engineering Works. It would give him great pleasure, Archilochos said, if Madame Georgette would also hang this picture of Petit-Paysan. Perhaps in place of Fahrcks. It seemed that the owner of the Engineering Works occupied the third place in Archilochos' ethical cosmos.

Madame Georgette bridled.

"Petit-Paysan manufactures machine guns," she said.

"What of it?"

"Tanks."

"What of it?"

"Atomic cannon."

"You forget the Petit-Paysan razor and the Petit-Paysan obstetrical forceps, Madame Bieler. Purely humanitarian products."

"Monsieur Archilochos," Georgette said solemnly, "I warn you against having anything more to do with Petit-Paysan."

"He is my employer," Arnolph replied.

Georgette laughed. "Then it doesn't do you a mite of good," she said, "to drink milk and mineral water, do without meat" (Archilochos was a vegetarian), "and keep away from women. Petit-Paysan supplies the army, and if the army builds up its armaments, there will be war. It has always been that way."

Archilochos did not agree.

"Not in our country!" he cried. "Not with our President!"

"Oh, him!"

Evidently she did not know about Petit-Paysan's Shelter for Expectant Mothers, Archilochos continued unabashed, and his Home for Disabled Workmen. Petit-Paysan was a highly ethical, truly Christian man.

But Madame Bieler refused to be swayed. The result was that his first two heroes shared a place on the wall with the man who stood lowest in Arnolph's ethical cosmos: the negative principle, Fahrcks, the Communist, who had instigated the coup d'état in San Salvador and the revolution in Borneo. Pale, shy, rather plump, Archilochos sat in his corner among the cycling fans with the portraits of only the first two of his exemplars on the wall. For he hadn't been able to persuade Georgette to hang Number Four in his cosmos either.

She might want to hang the picture underneath Fahrcks's, he had said, handing her a reproduction—a cheap one, incidentally.

"What artist painted that?" Georgette had asked, staring in bafflement at the triangular rectangles and the twisted circles in the reproduction.

"Passap."

It appeared that Monsieur Arnolph worshipped the world-famous painter. But what the picture was supposed to represent remained a mystery to Georgette.

"The right way of life," Archilochos told her.

"But it says *Chaos* down there," Georgette exclaimed, pointing to the lower right-hand corner of the painting.

Archilochos shook his head. "Great artists create unconsciously," he said. "I simply know that this picture represents the right way of life."

But Georgette was adamant. Archilochos was so offended that he did not turn up for three days. Then he began coming for his meals again, and in time Madame Bieler found out about the life of Monsieur Arnolph, insofar as it could be called a life, for it was all so punctual, well ordered, and screwy. Thus, for example, there was room in Archilochos' cosmos for Numbers Five to Eight.

Number Five was Bob Forster-Monroe, the American Ambassador. Though not an Old New Presbyterian of the Penultimate Christians, he was an Old Presbyterian of the Penultimate Christians—a painful but not hopeless difference which Archilochos, who was quite broadminded where religion was concerned, could discuss for hours at a time. (Aside from other churches, the only sect he resolutely rejected was the New Presbyterians of the Penultimate Christians.)

Number Six in the cosmos was Maître Dutour.

Number Seven was Hercule Wagner, Rector magnificus of the University.

Dutour had been the defense attorney for a sex murderer, eventually sentenced to be guillotined, who had been a curate of the Old New Presbyterians. This curate had sinned only in the flesh; his soul remained above the battle, uncontaminated, redeemed. The Rector magnificus, on the other hand, had visited the students' dormitory of the Penultimate Christians and chatted five minutes with Number Two in the cosmos (the Bishop).

Number Eight was Bibi Archilochos, Arnolph's brother—a good man, Arnolph maintained; he was unemployed, which surprised Georgette, for thanks to Petit-Paysan the country was booming.

Archilochos lived in a garret quite close to Chez Auguste, as the cycling star's little restaurant was called. It took him more than an hour to reach his place of work in the white twenty-story, Corbusier-designed administrative building of the Petit-Paysan Engineering Works, Inc. As for the garret: it was up five flights of stairs, a malodorous hallway, small, slanting ceiling, wallpaper of indeterminate design, a chair, a table, a bed, a Bible. In a curtained-off nook hung his Sunday suit. On the wall: first, President; second, Bishop; third, Petit-Paysan; fourth, reproduction of a painting by Passap (rectangular triangles); and so on down to Bibi—a family group, with his flock of children. View: a dirty wall no more than six feet away, a series of open, stinking little windows (belonging to the other building's toilets), the wall wildly splotched white, yellow, and green, transfigured by light from above only now and then, in midsummer, toward noon. Perpetual noise of toilets being flushed. As for his place of work: one of fifty other Bookkeepers in a mammoth room divided by glass partitions, labyrinthine, traversable only on the zigzag; on the seventh floor, Obstetrical Forceps Division, pencil behind his ear, gray work smock, its elbows reinforced with patches of leather; lunch in the canteen, where he pined for a picture of the President and the Bishop, but only Petit-Paysan hung there (Number Three). Archilochos was not a real Bookkeeper, only an Assistant Bookkeeper. Or, to be more precise: the Assistant Bookkeeper of an Assistant Bookkeeper. In short, one of the lowest of the Assistant Bookkeepers, insofar as it is possible to speak of a lowest, for the number of Bookkeepers and Assistant Bookkeepers in Petit-Paysan, Inc., was practically infinite. But even in this modest, this almost lowest job, he was still far better paid than the garret would have indicated. What had banished him to this dark den, flanked by toilets, was Bibi.

Madame Bieler

also made the acquaintance of Number Eight (the brother).

It was on a Sunday. Arnolph had invited Bibi Archilochos to dinner. Chez Auguste.

Bibi came with his wife, two mistresses, and seven little ones, the oldest of whom, Théophile and Gottlieb, were almost grown up. Magda-Maria, thirteen years old, brought along a lover. Bibi poved to be a hardened drinker; his wife was accompanied by "Uncle," as he was called: a retired sea captain who could not be got rid of. It was a rich spectacle, too rich even for the cycling fans. Théophile boasted of his session in the reformatory, Gottlieb of a bank robbery; Matthew and Sebastian, respectively twelve and nine years old, went around playfully threatening people with their knives; and the two youngest, the six-year-old twins, Jean-Christophe and Jean-Daniel, had a fight over a bottle of absinthe.

"What a bunch!" Georgette cried in horror after the devil's brood had finally cleared out of the establishment.

"Just youthful high spirits," Archilochos said to placate her. He paid the check—half a month's salary.

"Look here," Madame Bieler remonstrated, "that brother of yours seems to be raising a gang of criminals. You mean to say you give him money? Almost everything you earn?"

Archilochos' faith was unshakable. "One must always try to see the heart, Madame Bieler," he said. "And the heart is good. In every human being. Appearances are deceitful. My brother, his wife, and his dear little ones have an inner nobility, only life is a bit too much for them; they need help."

But now—it was a Sunday once again, half past nine in the morning—he entered the restaurant for different purposes. He had a red rose in his lapel. Georgette was impatiently awaiting him. It was really all the doing of the unceasing rain, the fogs, the cold, the constantly damp socks, and the epidemic of grippe, which in the course of time had changed into intestinal grippe—the result being that Archilochos (we know the location of his room) could not sleep for the constant gurgling roar. All this had gradually changed Arnolph's mind, as the water deepened in the gutters of the streets, and he had finally yielded to Madame Bieler's insistent urgings.

"You ought to get married, Monsieur Arnolph," she kept telling him. "This isn't any life for you, holed up in that garret of yours, or sitting around with cycling fans. A man with higher interests shouldn't live that way. You need a wife to take care of you."

"You take care of me, Madame Bieler."

"Oh come now, a wife is something completely different. A woman keeps a man snug and warm. You'll see."

At last she brought him round. He agreed to place a want ad in *Le Soir*. Georgette at once brought paper, pen, and ink to his table.

"Bachelor, Bookkeeper, forty-five, Old New Presbyterian, refined, seeks Old New Presbyterian wife . . ." she suggested.

"That wouldn't be necessary," Archilochos said. "I would convert my wife to the right faith."

Georgette granted that this was reasonable. "Seeks a loving wife, good disposition, own age, widow not excluded . . ."

She would have to be an innocent girl, Archilochos demurred.

Georgette would have none of that. "Put the idea of a girl out of your head," she told him. "You've never even been with a woman; one of you has to know how to do it."

The ad he had in mind was somewhat different, Monsieur Arnolph faltered.

"How would you write it?"

"GREEK SEEKS GREEK WIFE."

"*Mon Dieu,*" Madame Bieler exclaimed. "Don't tell me you're a Greek?" She stared at the plumpish, graceless, rather northern-looking frame of Monsieur Archilochos.

"You see, Madame Bieler," he replied shyly, "I know I hardly conform to the picture most people have of Greeks. It's a long time since my ancestor came to this country and died at the side of Charles the Bold in the Battle of Nancy. That's the reason I don't look much like a Greek. I admit it. But now, Madame Bieler, with this fog and cold and rain, I feel such a longing to return to my homeland, though I've never seen it. It usually comes over me in the wintertime—I long for the Peloponnesus, for the red cliffs and the blue sky—I've read all about it in *Match*. So if I were to get married, I'd want my bride to be a Greek, because she'd feel the same loneliness I feel in this country."

"You're a poet and no mistake," Georgette had replied, drying her eyes.

And sure enough, in two days Archilochos received an answer to his ad. A small, perfumed envelope; a card inside as blue as the sky of the Peloponnesus. Chloé Saloniki was writing to say that she was lonely and wished that she and he could meet.

With Georgette's coaching he wrote to Chloé: Chez Auguste, Sunday, January so and so. Identification: a red rose.

Archilochos had on the dark-blue suit he had worn to his confirmation, but had forgotten his overcoat. He was nervous. He wondered whether he should not turn back and hide in his garret. For the first time in his life be was irked when he found Bibi waiting for him in front of Chez Auguste, almost unrecognizable in the fog.

"Let me have a couple of centuries," Bibi said, extending his fraternal hand, palm upward. "Magda-Maria needs English lessons."

Archilochos expressed surprise.

"She's found herself a new steady," Bibi explained. "A hell of a nice guy, but he only speaks English."

Archilochos, red rose in his lapel, handed over the money.

Georgette, too, was in a state of suspense. Only Auguste seemed unperturbed; as was his custom when there were no guests in the restaurant, he sat by the stove in his cyclist's costume, rubbing his bare legs.

Madame Bieler wiped off the counter. "I wonder what she'll be like," she said. "Plump and pleasant is my guess. Not too old, I hope, though she doesn't mention her age on the card. But what woman likes to?"

Archilochos, shivering, ordered a cup of hot milk.

While he was cleaning his glasses, which had misted over from the steam of the milk, Chloé Saloniki entered the restaurant.

Nearsighted Archilochos at first saw Chloé only in outline, with a blotch of red somewhere to the right below the oval of the face—the rose, he surmised. But the silence that suddenly reigned over the place, this ghostly silence in which not the tinkle of a glass could be heard, nor the sound of anyone so much as drawing a breath, was so consternating that he did not instantly put on his glasses. In fact, as soon as he had, he snatched them off again and began to polish them in extreme excitement. It was unbelievable. A miracle had taken place, here in this little bistro, amid fog and rain. To this plumpish bachelor and timorous idealist, this prisoner of a stinking garret, barricaded behind his milk and mineral water, to this overscrupulous and overinhibited Assistant Bookkeeper of an Assistant Bookkeeper with his eternally damp and holey socks, his unironed shirt, ill-fitting clothes, worn shoes, and queer opinions, had come this good fairy, this vision of loveliness and grace, so perfect a little lady that Georgette did not dare stir and Auguste, abashed, hid his cyclist's legs behind the stove.

"Monsieur Archilochos?" a soft, hesitant voice inquired. Archilochos stood up, bumping his cuff into his cup, so that the milk spattered over his glasses. At last he managed to don them again, and through splashes of milk he blinked at Chloé Saloniki, frozen.

"Another cup of milk," he said at last.

"Oh," Chloé laughed. "I'd like one, too."

Archilochos sat down, unable to take his eyes off her or to invite her to take a seat, although he wanted to. He was terrified, depressed, and did not dare think of his ad. Miserably, he removed the rose from his lapel. He thought that any moment she would turn in disappointment and go away. Perhaps, too, he thought he was only dreaming. He had so quickly and so completely succumbed to the beauty of this girl, to the miracle of this moment, that he was utterly defenseless. It was incomprehensible, this wonder of wonders, and he dared not hope that it would last for more than a moment. He felt ridiculous and ugly; suddenly the condition of his garret loomed in all its enormity before him, the dreariness of the working-class district in which he lived, the monotony of his work as a Bookkeeper. But she simply sat down at the table opposite him and looked at him with enormous black eyes.

"Oh," she said happily, "I never imagined you would be so nice. I'm so pleased we Greeks have found each other. Come, let me have your glasses. There's milk all over them."

She took the glasses from his nose and wiped them with her scarf, or so it seemed to Archilochos, who could not see very well. She breathed on the glasses.

"Mademoiselle Saloniki," he at last choked out, as if pronouncing his own death sentence, "it may be I'm not quite a real Greek. My family emigrated in the days of Charles the Bold."

Chloé laughed. "Once a Greek, always a Greek."

Then she put his glasses on for him, and Auguste served them their milk.

"Mademoiselle Saloniki . . ."

"You must call me Chloé," she said. "Now that we're going to be married. I want to marry you because you're a Greek. My greatest desire is to make you happy."

Archilochos flushed. "This is the first time I've ever talked with a girl, Chloé," he said at last. "Up to now, my only contact with ladies has been with Madame Bieler."

Chloé did not reply. She seemed to be considering something, and the pair drank the hot, steaming milk.

After Chloé and Archilochos had left the restaurant together, Madame Bieler found her tongue again.

"What a looker," she said. "You wouldn't believe it. And that bracelet she was wearing, and her necklace— hundreds of thousands of francs. That girl must have worked! And did you see her coat. Some fur! A man couldn't want a finer wife."

"And so young," Auguste said, still staggered.

"Come on," Georgette replied, mixing herself a glass of Campari and soda, "she's seen thirty. But dolled up. I bet you she has herself massaged seven times a week."

"So did I," Auguste commented, "when I won the Tour de Suisse." He looked mournfully at his skinny legs.

"And some perfume!"

Chloé and Archilochos

stood in the street. It was still raining. The fog, too, still lurked in the air, and the cold that pierced through clothing.

"There's a temperance restaurant opposite the World Health Office." he said at last. "Very reasonable."

He shivered in his damp and threadbare confirmation suit.

"Won't you give me your arm?" Chloé asked him.

The Assistant Bookkeeper was embarrassed. He did not quite know how it was done. He scarcely dared to look at the vision tripping along beside him through the fog, with a silvery blue scarf thrown over her black hair. He felt rather uneasy. This was the first time he had ever walked through the city with a girl, and so he was actually grateful for the fog. A church bell struck half past ten. They walked through deserted suburban streets, whose buildings were mirrored in the wet asphalt. Their footsteps echoed from the walls of houses. It was as if they were passing through an underground vault. Not a person was in sight. A half-starved dog trotted toward them out of the gloom, a dirty black-and-white spaniel, dripping with wetness, with drooping ears and dropping tongue. The red lights at intersections shimmered through the mist. Then a bus rolled past, pointlessly sounding its horn, evidently headed for North Station. Archilochos pressed his head into the soft fur of her coat, to find room under her dainty red umbrella. He was overwhelmed by the deserted street, the Sunday, the weather. They walked along in step, almost like a regular pair of lovers. Somewhere the Salvation Army was singing nasally in the fog, and now and then the Télédiffusion's Sunday-morning concert could be heard coming from a house—some symphony or other, Beethoven or Schubert, mingled with the tooting of automobiles lost in the fog. The two of them were drifting toward the river, they guessed, through uniform streets, only snatches of which were disclosed as it grew somewhat brighter, though everything was still swathed in grayness. Then they walked along an endless boulevard past monotonously similar façades, which now showed clearly through the mist, past the villas of long-since ruined bankers and faded cocottes, with Doric and Corinthian columns at the doors, with stiff balconies and tall windows on the second floor, most of them illuminated, most of them battered, phantomlike, dripping.

Chloé began to tell the story of her life, which was as wondrous as she herself. She spoke shyly, haltingly. But to the Assistant Bookkeeper, everything fantastic seemed perfectly natural. After all, he was living a fairy tale.

She was an orphan, she said, her parents poor wanderers from Crete who had frozen to death in the terrible winters. In barracks. That was the beginning of the great loneliness. She grew up in the slums, unkempt, ragged, just like that black-and-white spaniel, had stolen fruit and robbed poor boxes. The police hounded her. Procurers pursued her. She slept under bridges, among tramps and in empty barrels, shy and suspicious as a wild animal. Then she was picked up, literally that is, by an archaeological couple out for an evening walk, and placed in a convent school. At present she was living as a maid in the home of her benefactors, was decently dressed, decently fed—a touching story, all in all.

"An archaeological couple?" Arnolph asked wonderingly. He had never heard of anything of the sort.

"A couple who studied archaeology," Chloé Saloniki explained, "and who had made excavations in Greece. They discovered a temple there, with precious statues, buried in a bog, and golden columns."

What was their name?

Chloé hesitated. She seemed to be seeking a name.

"Gilbert and Elizabeth Weeman."

"The famous Weemans?"

(An article on them with colored photos had just appeared in *Match*.)

"Yes."

He would incorporate them into his ethical cosmos, Arnolph said. As Numbers Nine and Ten. Or perhaps as Numbers Six and Seven, with Maître Dutour and the Rector magnificus shifted to Numbers Nine and Ten—still positions of considerable honor.

"You have an ethical cosmos?" Chloé asked in astonishment. "What in the world is that?"

A man must have something to lean on in life, ethical models, Archilochos said. He, too, had not had an easy life, although he had not grown up among murderers and tramps, as she had done, but only with his brother Bibi in an orphanage. And he began describing to her the structure of his moral universe.

The weather had changed

although at first they scarcely noticed. The rain had stopped and the fog was lifting. It turned into ghostly figures, long, sinuous dragons, clumsy bears, and giant men that slid over houses, banks, and government buildings, intertwining, rising, and dissolving. Blue sky shimmered between masses of fog, delicate and elusive at first, a mere hint of spring, which was still months away, faintly tinged by sunlight, then clearer, brighter, stronger. Suddenly the wet asphalt was printed with the reflections of buildings, street lamps, monuments, people, and the city burst forth with superclarity, bathed in the flood of new light.

They were on the Quai in front of the President's Palace. The river had swollen to a brown torrent. Spanning it were bridges with rusty iron railings; empty barges, hung with diapers, moved downstream, while shivering skippers, smoking pipes, paced up and down their decks. The streets now swarmed with strollers, dignified grandfathers accompanied by grandchildren in their Sunday best, families marching in solid rows down the sidewalks. There were many policemen about, and reporters obviously waiting for the President, who now came charging out of the palace in his historic chariot, drawn by six white horses, accompanied by his mounted bodyguard with their golden helmets and white plumes. He was off to perform some political act somewhere, to dedicate a monument, pin a medal on someone's chest, or open an orphanage. The tramp of hooves, blare of trumpets and drums, cheers, and hats filled the rain-washed air.

Then the incomprehensible happened.

The President rode past Chloé and Archilochos. Arnolph, overjoyed at this unexpected meeting with Number One in his cosmos, which he was just explaining, peered at the goateed, gray-haired dignitary who sat, resplendent in gold braid, framed by the window of his carriage, just like the picture that hung above Madame Bieler's bottles of Pernod and Campari. And just at this moment the President suddenly greeted the Assistant Bookkeeper. His Excellency waved his right hand just as if Archilochos were an old acquaintance. So conspicuous was this fluttering motion of a white glove, and so plainly was it intended for him, that two policemen with impressive mustaches snapped to attention in front of Archilochos.

"The President greeted me," Archilochos stammered incredulously.

"Why shouldn't he greet you?" Chloé Saloniki asked.

"But I'm only an insignificant ordinary citizen."

"But isn't the President the father of us all?" Chloé suggested.

Almost immediately there took place another episode which Archilochos could not understand, but which filled him with fresh pride.

He was just about to speak of Number Two in his cosmos, Bishop Moser, and of the vital difference between the Old New and the Old Presbyterians of the Penultimate Christians, with a brief mention of the New Presbyterians (that scandal within the Presbyterian Church)—he was just about to speak of all this when, out of turn, Number Three of the cosmos met them: Petit-Paysan. He must have come either from the World Bank, five hundred yards away from the President's Palace, or from St. Luke's Cathedral, which adjoined the World Bank. He was dressed in an immaculate coat, top hat, and white scarf, fairly crackling with elegance. His chauffeur had already opened the door of the Rolls-Royce when Arnolph caught sight of him. Arnolph did not know quite what to do.

This event was unique, and would serve to illustrate the explanations he was at this moment giving Chloé about his cosmos. The great industrialist did not know Archilochos, could not possibly know him who was only an Assistant Bookkeeper in the Obstetrical Forceps Division. But that very fact gave Archilochos the courage to point out this superior being, though not to greet him (one does not greet a god). And so, though frightened, Archilochos felt safe in the consciousness that he could pass by this man of might unrecognized. But for the second time the incomprehensible thing happened: Petit-Paysan smiled, doffed his top hat, waved it, bowed graciously to a pale Archilochos, then dropped into the upholstery of his limousine, waved once more, and roared off.

"But that was Petit-Paysan!" Archilochos panted.

"So what?"

"Number Three in my cosmos."

"What about him?"

"He greeted me!"

"I should hope so."

"But I'm only an Assistant Bookkeeper and work with fifty other Assistant Bookkeepers in the lowest department of the Obstetrical Forceps Division," Archilochos exclaimed.

"Then he must be a man with a social conscience," Chloé declared, "worthy of holding third place in your moral universe."

Evidently she did not really grasp the truly amazing nature of this meeting.

But the wonders of this Sunday had not yet ceased. The weather, in the middle of winter, grew steadily warmer and more brilliant, the sky steadily bluer and more unreal, and the whole metropolis seemed suddenly determined to greet Archilochos as he strolled, his Greek girl at his side, over the bridges with their wrought-iron railings and through the gardens and parks outside the decaying castles. Arnolph became prouder, more self-assured, his gait freer, his face radiant. He was more than an Assistant Bookkeeper now. He was a happy man. Fashionable young fellows hailed him, waved from cafés, buses, and Vespas. So did *soigné* gentlemen with graying temples, and even a Belgian general with many decorations, evidently attached to NATO headquarters, who was getting out of a jeep. In front of the American Embassy, Ambassador Bob Forster-Monroe, accompanied by two Scotch sheep dogs, called out a hearty "hello"; while Number Two (Bishop Moser, who looked even more well-fed in the flesh than he did in the picture hanging in Madame Bieler's bistro) encountered them between the National Museum and the crematorium, as they were about to enter the temperance restaurant opposite the World Health Office. Bishop Moser also greeted him. By now this somehow seemed only right and proper, although Archilochos did not know him personally at all, had only sat in a crowd of hymn-singing females listening to him preach the Easter sermon. However, Archilochos had read his biography at least a hundred times, in the pamphlet on this exemplary personage which was distributed among the congregation. The Bishop seemed even more startled than the lowly member of his Old New Presbyterian Church, for he scurried down an absurd side street with remarkable haste.

Then they dined together in the temperance restaurant. They sat at a window table and looked out across the river at the World Health Office with the monument to a famous World Health official in front of it, on which the gulls rested, rose, swooped around, and rested again. They were both tired from the long walk, and they continued merely to sit and hold hands even after the soup had been placed before them. The restaurant was mainly patronized by Old New Presbyterians (and a scattering of Old Presbyterians), mostly spinsters and eccentric bachelors who came to dine here on Sundays for the cause of temperance, although the proprietor, an obstinate Catholic, stubbornly refused to hang Bishop Moser's portrait. On the contrary, the Archbishop hung beside the President.

Later, they sat,

two Greeks beneath two Greeks, moving closer and closer to each other, on a bench in the old municipal park under a mildewed statue which was described, by guides and city maps, as representing Daphnis and Chloé. They watched the sun drop behind the trees, a red child's balloon. Here, too, everyone greeted Archilochos. Usually only cycling fans and Assistant Bookkeepers noticed him; but now this pallid, bespectacled, plumpish, and altogether inconspicuous man seemed to interest the entire city, to be the center of society. The fairy tale went on. Number Four (Passap) passed by, followed by a band of bewildered or enthusiastic art critics, for the master had just abandoned his rectangular period with its circles and hyperbolas and was now painting only angles of sixty degrees with ellipses and parabolas, and from red and green had turned to cobalt blue and ocher. The master of modern painting came to a stop, growled, looked keenly at Archilochos, nodded, and strolled on, continuing his lecture to the critics. On the other hand, the former Numbers Six and Seven (now Nine and Ten), Maître Dutour and the Rector magnificus, greeted Archilochos with a barely perceptible wink, for they were walking at the side of imposing wives.

Archilochos told Chloé about his life. "I don't earn very much," he said. "The work is monotonous; it involves checking over the reports on our obstetrical forceps, and calls for the utmost care and precision. My superior, a Vice Bookkeeper, is strict, and I also have to support my brother Bibi and his dear little ones, lovable people, perhaps a little rough and wild, but good at heart. We will save, and in twenty years we'll be able to visit Greece together. The Peloponnesus. The islands. I've dreamed of that for ever so long, and now that I know I'll go there with you, the dream has become even more beautiful."

She said she was thrilled. "It will be a lovely trip," she said.

"On an ocean liner."

"On the *Julia*."

He looked inquiringly at her.

"That's a luxury ship. Mrs. and Mr. Weeman sail on it."

"Of course," he recalled, "I read about that in *Match*. But the *Julia* will be too expensive for us, and in twenty years they'll have scrapped it. We'll go on a freighter. They're cheaper."

He often thought about Greece, he went on, looking out at the fog, which was beginning to settle in again, drifting down toward the ground like thin white smoke. He could see the broken pillars of the ancient temples, and the red cliffs shimmering through the olive groves. "Sometimes I feel I am in exile in this city, like the Jews in Babylon, and that the whole meaning of my life is to return someday to the old homeland my ancestors abandoned so long ago."

Now the fog lay like great heaps of cotton batting behind the trees by the banks of the river, swaddling the slow-moving barges, which howled ruttishly. The masses of fog rose, flared violet, and began to spread as soon as the big red sun had dropped below the horizon. Archilochos escorted Chloé to the boulevard where the Weemans lived—a fine expensive neighborhood, he noted. They passed wrought-iron fences, big gardens with noble old trees which screened the houses from the public view. Poplars, elms, beeches, and black fir trees towered into the silvery evening sky, their tops vanishing in the thickening billows of fog. Chloé stopped in front of an iron gate decorated with putti and dolphins, exotic foliage and arabesques, flanked by two huge stone pillars and surmounted by a red lamp.

"Tomorrow night?"

"Chloé!"

"Will you ring?" she asked, pointing to an old-fashioned bellpull. "At eight?"

Then she kissed the Assistant Bookkeeper. She put her arms around his neck, kissed him once more, then a third time.

"We'll go to Greece," she whispered. "To our old homeland. Soon. And on the *Julia*."

She opened the iron gate and vanished into the mist among the trees, waving to him once more and calling out something, some tender phrase, like a mysterious bird as she walked toward some invisible building deep in the spacious garden.

Archilochos, for his part, trudged back to his working-class neighborhood. It was a long walk; he retraced the whole route he had taken with Chloé. And he thought over the phases of this fabulous Sunday, stood still on the deserted sidewalk in front of the closed-up World Bank, beneath Daphnis and Chloé, then in front of the temperance restaurant, which the last of the Old New Presbyterian spinsters were just leaving. One of them greeted him, and perhaps waited for him on the next street corner. Then he walked past the crematorium, the National Museum, and the Quai. The fog was thick again, but not dirty as it had been on previous days; it was soft and milky, a miraculous fog, it seemed to him, shot through with long golden rays of light, with delicate, needlelike stars. He reached the Ritz, and as he passed the pompous portal with its six-foot doorman in green coat and red trousers and carrying a long silver staff, Gilbert and Elizabeth Weeman emerged from the hotel. He recognized the world-famous archaeologists from their pictures in the newspapers. They were both exceedingly English; she looked more like a man than a woman, with her hair cut short just like her husband's, and both had pince-nez. The only salient difference was that Gilbert had a red mustache and stubby pipe.

Archilochos plucked up his courage. "Madame, monsieur," he said. "My respects."

"Well," the scientist said, staring at the Assistant Bookkeeper, who stood before him in his threadbare confirmation suit and down-at-heel shoes. Mrs. Weeman likewise examined him through her pince-nez.

"Well," Mr. Weeman said again. And then he added: "Yes?"

"I have appointed you Numbers Six and Seven in my ethical cosmos."

"Yes?"

"You have given a home to a Greek girl," Archilochos continued.

"Well," Mr. Weeman said.

"I, too, am a Greek."

"Oh," Mr. Weeman said, taking out his wallet.

Archilochos made a gesture of refusal. "No, monsieur, no, madame," he said. "I know I do not look very trustworthy, and perhaps not even Greek, but my salary at the Petit-Paysan Engineering Works will suffice for me to set up a modest household with her. Yes, we will even be able to think of starting a family, though only of three or four, because the Petit-Paysan Engineering Works maintains an excellent maternity clinic for its employees."

"Well," Mr. Weeman said, pocketing his wallet.

"Good-by," Archilochos said. "God bless you. I will pray for you in the Old New Presbyterian Church."

But at the door

of his house he met Bibi, whose brotherly hand was extended, palm upward.

"Théophile was trying a snatch in the National Bank," he said in his argot. "The bulls caught wise."

"So?"

"He has to beat it to the south till things quiet down. I need five centuries. You'll have 'em back at Christmas."

Archilochos gave him money.

"What's this, Brother," Bibi protested in disappointment. "No more than a tenner?"

"I can't give you any more, Bibi," Archilochos apologized, embarrassed and, to his surprise, a little annoyed. "Really not. I had dinner with a girl in the temperance restaurant opposite the World Health Office. The regular Sunday dinner and a bottle of grape juice besides. I'm thinking about starting a family of my own."

Brother Bibi looked alarmed.

"What do you want with a family?" he cried out indignantly. "I've got one already. Does the chick have any money at least?"

"No."

"What line she in?"

"She works for some rich people as housemaid."

"Where?"

"Number 12 Boulevard Saint-Père."

Bibi whistled through his teeth.

"Go hit the hay, Arnolph, but lemme have another tenner."

After climbing the six flights of stairs to his garret, Archilochos undressed. He went to bed. He wished he could open the window. The air was stale. But the toilets were more odoriferous than usual. He lay in semi-darkness. Lights went on and off, first in one narrow little window, then in another, across the area-way. The roar of flushing never stopped. Alternately lights flashed against the wall of his room, illuminating one of the pictures in his ethical cosmos, now the Bishop, now the President, now Bibi with his little brood, now the triangular rectangles in Passap's painting, now one of the other figures.

"Tomorrow I must obtain a photograph of the Weemans and have it framed," he mused.

The air was so stuffy that he could hardly breathe. Sleep was out of the question. He had gone to bed happy, but now worries descended. It would be impossible to live in this garret with Chloé, to found a household, to accommodate the three or four dear little children he had planned for on the way home. He must find new lodgings. But he had no money for a better place, no savings. He had given all he earned to Brother Bibi. He owned nothing. Not even this wretched bed, the miserable table, and the rickety stool. It all belonged to the landlord of this furnished room. Only the pictures which comprised his moral cosmos were his own property. His poverty weighed on him. Chloé's delicacy and beauty called for beautiful and delicate surroundings, he sensed. She must never again return to the bridges by the river and the empty barrels at garbage dumps. The roar of the flushing toilets began to strike him as more and more malignant, more and more repulsive. He vowed to leave this garret. Tomorrow, he decided, he would look for another apartment. But as he considered how he would go about moving, a feeling of helplessness overcame him. He saw no way. He realized that he was caught in a merciless machine, without any way to make anything of the miracle that had been offered to him this glorious Sunday. Drearily, in complete despair, he lay awake waiting for morning, which at last announced its coming with an intensified thunder of water closets.

Toward eight o'clock, as on every Monday morning
—and at this time of year it was still dark—Archilochos hustled into the administrative offices of the
Petit-Paysan Engineering Works. He was one more in
an army of Bookkeepers, stenographers, and Assistant
Bookkeepers, an insignificant particle in the gray
stream of humanity which poured out of the subway,
the buses, the streetcars, and the suburban railroad
cars, and flowed sadly toward the gigantic steel-and-
glass cube which swallowed, divided, and sorted them
out, pushed them up and down elevators and escala-
tors, crowded them along corridors. First floor: Tank
Division. Second floor: Atomic Cannon. Third floor:
Machine Gun Division. And so on. Archilochos,
wedged among the crowds, pushed around and shoved
about, worked on the seventh floor, Obstetrical Forceps Division. Office 122-OF, in one of the many fea-
tureless spaces partitioned off with glass walls. Before
he entered, however, he had to step into the Hygiene
Room, gargle, and take a pill (against intestinal
grippe); these measures were required by Social Wel-
fare. Then he put on his gray working smock, still
shivering; for the first intense, cutting frost of winter
had descended overnight, laying a light, smooth polish
over all surfaces. He had to hurry, for it was already a
minute before eight and lateness was not tolerated

(time is money). He sat down at a desk, likewise of steel and glass, which he shared with three other Assistant Bookkeepers, who bore numbers, AB122-OF28, AB122-OF29, AB122-OF30, and uncovered his typewriter. The number on his smock was AB122-OF31. Fingers still stiff, he began to type; the hand of the big clock had moved to eight. This morning he had to complete a summary of the upsurge in obstetrical forceps sales in the Canton of Appenzell Inner Rhoden.

Like himself, the three other Assistant Bookkeepers at his desk clattered away at their typewriters, and the forty-six others in the room, the hundreds, thousands in the building, from eight to twelve and from two to five, with meals in the Works Canteen in between. It was all part of the exemplary Petit-Paysan organization, which was so often visited by cabinet ministers, foreign delegations, bespectacled Chinese, and sensuous Hindus, who, having an interest in social conditions, floated through the big rooms, silken wives at their sides.

But sometimes, though seldom, the miracles of Sunday continue on Monday.

_44_

An announcement

came over the loudspeaker, telling Archilochos to report to his office head, Bookkeeper B121-OF. For a moment there was deathly silence in Room 122-OF. Not a breath could be heard. Not the timid click of a single typewriter key. The Greek stood up. Pale, reeling. He had a foreboding of bad news. Dismissals were impending.

But Bookkeeper B121-OF received him in his office, which adjoined 122-OF, with real cordiality, as Archilochos discovered to his amazement; he had halted on the threshold, hardly daring to enter, for awful stories went the rounds of B121-OF's outbursts of temper.

"Monsieur Archilochos," B121-OF called out, striding forward to meet the Assistant Bookkeeper and actually shaking his hand, "I have been keeping my eye on your remarkable talents for a long time, I must say."

"Oh, thank you," Archilochos said, surprised at the praise and still on guard.

B121-OF rubbed his hands. He was a small, nimble chap of fifty, bald, with nearsighted eyes, dressed in a white Bookkeeper's smock with gray elbow pads. "Your follow-up on the distribution and maintenance standards of obstetrical forceps in the canton of Appenzell Inner Rhoden is exemplary."

He was glad to hear that, Archilochos said, still certain that he was the candidate for some cruel whim on the Bookkeeper's part, and that this friendliness was only a trick.

The Bookkeeper offered his suspicious assistant a chair, and began nervously pacing his office.

"In view of your excellent work, my dear Monsieur Archilochos, I have been planning to take certain steps."

"I am greatly honored," Archilochos stammered.

He had been thinking of promotion to the post of Vice Bookkeeper, B121-OF murmured. "I have just sent the proposal to the Chief of Personnel responsible for our office."

Archilochos stood up, with an appropriate look of gratitude; but the Bookkeeper had still another matter on his mind. He looked anxious and unhappy as he came out with it, just as if he were an Assistant Bookkeeper.

"I'd almost forgotten," B121-OF said softly, trying

not to show his emotion, "Chief Bookkeeper CB9-OF wishes to see Monsieur Archilochos. This very morning."

The Bookkeeper wiped the sweat from his brow with a red checked handkerchief.

"The Chief Bookkeeper," he continued, "wishes to see you right away. Sit down again, my dear friend; we have another minute. Above all, collect yourself, don't lose your nerve, take courage, meet the situation like a man."

"Certainly," Archilochos said. "I'll try."

"Good Lord," his superior said, seating himself behind his desk. "Good Lord, Monsieur Archilochos, I'm sure I may call you my good friend, in confidence and just between the two of us—my name is Rummel, Emil Rummel. This is an event. It has never happened to me before, and I have been working in the Petit-Paysan Engineering Works for thirty-three years. A Chief Bookkeeper wishes to see an Assistant Bookkeeper, just like that. Never in my life have I seen such a dramatic jump outside of the regular channels. I feel faint, my dear friend. Of course, I believed in your brilliance all along, but still. Why, never in my whole life have I stood in the presence of a Chief Bookkeeper; I'd tremble like an aspen leaf if I did. A Bookkeeper deals only with Vice Chief Bookkeepers, of course!

And now this happening to you! Being interviewed by a Chief Bookkeeper! No doubt there are reasons for it, a secret intent. I foresee a promotion; you will receive my post, that's it" (at this point B121-OF dried his eyes). "Perhaps you'll even be made Vice Chief Bookkeeper, as happened recently in the Atomic Cannon Division to a Bookkeeper who had the honor to become somewhat intimate with the wife of a Chief of Personnel—I'm not referring to you, my friend, not you—in your case it's only your ability, that marvelous report on Appenzell Inner Rhoden, I know. But just between you and me, my dear friend: It was only by sheer chance that my proposal to promote you to Vice Bookkeeper and the summons from the Chief Bookkeeper came at virtually the same moment. I give you my word of honor, that's the case. My petition for your promotion was already written when out of a clear sky the telephone call from our respected Chief Bookkeeper's secretary reached me. But it's time, it's time, my good friend—incidentally my wife would be delighted to have you to dinner— my daughter likewise, very charming, very pretty, takes singing lessons—if you'd care to—if you'd do us the honor—fifth corridor southeast, sixth office—good Lord, and my heart isn't what it should be—trouble with my kidneys, too."

CB9-OF,

fifth corridor southeast, sixth office, a substantial man with neatly trimmed black beard, flashing gold teeth, paunch, and odor of cologne water, the photograph of a scantily clad dancer in a platinum frame on his desk, received the Assistant Bookkeeper with respect, shooed flocks of stenographers out of his office, and with an expansive wave of his hand offered his caller a comfortable easy chair.

"My dear Monsieur Archilochos," he began, "your excellent reports have attracted notice among our staff of Chief Bookkeepers for some time, especially your study of the new market for obstetrical forceps in the Far North, with special attention to Alaska. Your charts have created a sensation, have, I may say, evoked a storm of admiration. There has been much discussion of the matter within our circles, and word has gone around that the Directors have also been enormously impressed."

"There must be some mistake, sir," Arnolph demurred. "I deal only with the canton of Appenzell Inner Rhoden and the Tyrol."

"Just call me Petit-Pierre," CB9-OF said. "After all, we're among ourselves here, not in a crowd of philistines. Whether or not the Alaska report was written by you, it was inspired by you, breathes your spirit, reflects the incomparable style of your classical reports on the canton of Appenzell Inner Rhoden and the Tyrol. One more happy sign that your work is setting the tone. I always used to exclaim to my colleague Chief Bookkeeper Schränzle: Archilochos is a writer, a great prose stylist. Incidentally, Schränzle sends his regards. As does Chief Bookkeeper Häberlin. I have long been disturbed over the subordinate post you occupy in our esteemed organization, a post entirely out of keeping with your remarkable abilities. By the way, may I offer you a glass of vermouth . . . ?"

"Thank you, Monsieur Petit-Pierre," Archilochos said. "I am a teetotaler."

"It seems to me a particular scandal that you should be working under Bookkeeper B121-OF, Monsieur Rummler, or whatever his name is. There's a true mediocrity for you."

"He has just proposed my promotion to Vice Bookkeeper."

"I wouldn't put it past him," CB9-OF said irately. "Vice Bookkeeper indeed! He'd like that! A man of your talent! Why, the Petit-Paysan Engineering Works owes the surge in obstetrical forceps production during the last quarter entirely to you."

"But Monsieur Petit-Pierre . . ."

"Don't be too modest, my dear sir, don't be too modest. Everything has its limits. Here I've been waiting patiently for years, hoping that you would turn to me in confidence as your most faithful friend and admirer, and you simply go on sticking it out under that unbearable, low-minded Bookkeeper, staying on as an Assistant Bookkeeper among Assistant Bookkeepers, in an environment that really doesn't suit you at all. Instead of pounding your fist on the table! It must have been sheer hell to be with that beastly crew. So I've had to intervene directly. Of course I'm only a helpless little Chief Bookkeeper in the labyrinth of our administration, a cipher, a zero. But I've screwed up my courage. After all, someone had to speak up for you, no matter if the world comes to an end, no matter if it costs him his own head. Pluck, my dear fellow! If we don't have that, the moral fiber of the Petit-Paysan Engineering Works is gone and what have we left but down-and-out tyranny of bureaucracy, as I've been yelling all my life. I telephoned personally to the Chief of Personnel of our division, who incidentally sends his regards to you. I wanted to propose you as Vice Director; fact is, I couldn't think of anything finer than continuing to work under you, my dear Monsieur Archilochos, serving our common cause, the constant improvement and widening market for obstetrical forceps. But Petit-Paysan himself, Our Father in Heaven, as it were, or destiny, if you will, has alas, alas, anticipated me—a bit of personal ill luck which, of course, as far as you're concerned, represents a great though not undeserved good fortune."

"Petit-Paysan?" Archilochos thought he was dreaming. "But that's simply impossible!"

"He wants to see you today, this very morning, this very hour, Monsieur Archilochos," CB9-OF said.

"But . . ."

"No buts."

"I mean . . ."

"Monsieur Archilochos," the Chief Bookkeeper said earnestly, running his hand down his well-tended beard, "let us speak frankly with one another. As man to man, as friend to friend. I tell you in all honesty: This is a historic day, a day of candor, of clarification. My whole soul demands that I assure you, on my word of honor, that the fact that I have proposed you for Vice Director and the fact that our revered Petit-

Paysan, hats off to him, wishes to see you, have nothing whatsoever to do with one another. On the contrary. I had just dictated the formal proposal for your promotion when Director Zeus sent for me."

"Director Zeus?"

"Head of the Obstetrical Forceps Division."

Archilochos apologized for his ignorance. He had never heard the name.

"I know," the Chief Bookkeeper replied, "the names of Directors have not reached down to the circles of Bookkeepers and Assistant Bookkeepers. What would be the point? Such coolies are supposed to keep scribbling, composing drivel on the canton of Appenzell Inner Rhoden or God knows what out-of-the-way corners of the world that between you and me, my dear Monsieur Archilochos, nobody gives a damn about—your papers excepted, of course—we rely on them, we Chief Bookkeepers can't wait to read them. But then your reports on the canton of Basel or Costa Rica are magnificent, classics, as I've already said. As for the rest—overpaid, useless buffoons, all those Bookkeepers and Assistant Bookkeepers. I've been trying to get that across to my superiors in the administration for ages. I'd do the work of that whole crew with my stenographers alone. The Petit-Paysan Engineering Works isn't a sanatorium for morons. Incidentally, Director Zeus wishes me to give you his regards."

"Thank you."

"Unfortunately he's in the hospital now."

"Oh."

"Nervous breakdown."

"I'm sorry to hear that."

"You see, my dear friend, you've introduced sheer disaster into the upper echelons of the Obstetrical Forceps Division. Sodom and Gomorrah were a harmless little bonfire by comparison. Petit-Paysan wants to see you! Very well, that's his right, the Lord can turn the moon into green cheese if He likes, but all the same we'd be taken aback if He did. Petit-Paysan and an Assistant Bookkeeper! It's about the same kind of miracle. No wonder the poor Director heard the bell tolling. And the Vice Director? He went to pieces too."

"But why?"

"My dear sir, because you are going to be appointed Director of the Obstetrical Forceps Division. Any child can see that. Otherwise there'd be no point to all this. When Petit-Paysan sends for a man, he is slated for the directorship. We know what we know. Firing is done by the Chief of Personnel."

"Director? Me?"

"Certainly. The promotion has already been communicated to Personnel Chief Feuz, who incidentally also asks me to give you his regards."

"Of the Obstetrical Forceps Division?"

"Possibly of the Atomic Cannon Division also. Who knows? Personnel Chief Feuz thinks anything is possible."

"But why in the world?" Archilochos cried out. Nothing made sense.

"My dear, dear fellow! You forget your distinguished reports on Upper Italy . . ."

His territory was eastern Switzerland and the Tyrol, the Assistant Bookkeeper obstinately repeated.

"Eastern Switzerland and the Tyrol—I mix places up—I'm not a geographer, you know."

"But that can't be a reason for appointing me Director of Obstetrical Forceps."

"Come now!"

"I don't have the qualities for a Director," Archilochos protested.

CB9-OF shook his head and threw a mysterious look at Archilochos. He smiled, flashing his gold teeth, and folded his hands over his impressive paunch. "The reason," he said, "my dearest, my most honored friend, the reason you are being promoted to the directorship is something you must know, not I. And if you do not know it, don't try to find out. It's better that way. Take my advice. This is probably the last time we will sit face to face. Directors and Chief Bookkeepers do not ordinarily associate; that would be a breach of the unwritten rules of our great firm. Why, I myself met Director Zeus for the first time today, in the hour of his downfall, to be sure. And that was only because poor Vice Director Stüssi, who is my proper superior and who alone associates with Chief Bookkeepers, was being carried out on a stretcher. Truly, a twilight of the gods. But let us pass over this memorable scene in silence. As for your scruples, your fears that you cannot manage the métier of a Director—my dearest friend, between you and me, anybody can master the métier of a Director. Any idiot can do it. All you need do is simply be the Director, exist as Director, assume the dignity, represent the company, lead Indians, Chinese, and Zulus through the building, show around members of UNESCO and medical associations and anybody else in God's great world who is interested in that noble instrument the obstetrical forceps. The practical affairs, the plant, the technology, the computations, the market research—all that is handled by the Chief Bookkeepers, if I may express myself rather candidly to an honored friend. No need for you to grow any gray hairs over that. What will be important, of course, is whom you pick from the ranks of the Chief Bookkeepers to be Vice Director. Stüssi's finished now, you see, and high time too; the man was too closely linked with Director Zeus, nothing but His Lordship's tool—but, well, I don't want to express an opinion on Zeus's professional qualifications. Wouldn't be right at this point. He has his nervous breakdown. Far be it from me to criticize. Though it was a cross working under him, just between you and me. Why, the man was totally incapable of comprehending the reports on Dalmatia which you composed, my dearest friend and respected patron. And in general, the man hadn't a glimmer—I know, I know, it wasn't Dalmatia, it was Toggenburg or Turkey. Let's forget that. You were born for higher things. Like an eagle, you soar above the heads of us wonder-struck Chief Bookkeepers, into the empyrean. At any rate, just this one more confidential remark: We Chief Bookkeepers are delighted to have you as our Director! I don't even want to stress that as your best friend I particularly will sing hallelujah and hosannah" (at this point CB9-OF's eyes grew moist); "it really wouldn't do, would seem as if I were angling for the post of Vice Director, although of course I do have seniority. Whatever your choice among us Chief

Bookkeepers, whomever you appoint to be your deputy, I shall accept the decision with humility and remain your greatest admirer. . . . Colleague Spätzle would like a chance to see you, and then colleague Schränzle, but I'm afraid, I'm afraid, I must now take you to Petit-Paysan without more ado, deliver you undamaged to his waiting room, it's growing late. So come now, head up, enjoy your good fortune; after all, you are the worthiest, the most talented of all of us, a golden boy, so to speak, born under a bright star. The Obstetrical Forceps Division will outstrip the Machine Gun Division with colors flying, I predict. My dear sir, dear Director Archilochos, as I may as well address you from now on, would you do me the honor of coming with me, it's a great pleasure, we may as well take the Directors' elevator right away."

With CB9-OF,

Archilochos entered rooms whose existence he had never suspected, realms of glass and unknown materials, sparkling with cleanliness; superb elevators which bore him to the upper, mysterious stories of the administration building. Pretty stenographers swept fragrantly past, smiling, blonde, brunette, and raven, and one with glorious vermilion hair. Male secretaries made way for him, Directors bowed, General Directors nodded; velvety corridors received him, the red or green lights blinking over their doors the only signs of discreet administrative activity. They walked soundlessly on soft carpets; all noise, even the slightest clearing of throats or suppressed coughs, seemed banned from these regions. French Impressionists glowed on the walls (Petit-Paysan's collection of paintings was famous); a dancer by Degas, a bather by Renoir. Flowers in tall vases exuded their scents. The higher they mounted, the fewer people they encountered in the corridors and rooms, which ceased to be functional, supermodern, and cold, though their proportions remained the same. The ambience here was more imaginative, warmer, more human; the walls were tapestried, hung with gilded rococo and Louis Quatorze mirrors, a few Poussins, a sprinkling of Watteaus, a Claude Lorrain. And when they reached the topmost floor (CB9-OF, by now as overawed as Archilochos, for he had never penetrated so far, bid good-by at this point), the Assistant Bookkeeper was received by a stately gray-haired gentleman in faultless dinner jacket, probably a secretary, who led him down peaceful corridors and through big, bright rooms filled with antique vases and Gothic madonnas, Asiatic idols and Indian hangings. Here was no reminder at all of the manufacture of atomic cannon and machine guns, though possibly the sight of a few cherubic babes and dwarfs, which smiled at Archilochos out of a Rubens painting, might remotely call to mind obstetrical forceps. Everything was bright and serene in these altitudes. The sun was a magnanimous disk shining warmly through the windows, although in reality it stood in an icy sky. Comfortable easy chairs and sofas stood about. Somewhere hearty laughter could be heard; it reminded Archilochos, in his gray working smock, of Chloé's laughter on the bright Sunday which was now having so fabulous a continuation. Somewhere music trembled in the air, Haydn or Mozart; there was no clattering of typewriters, no rushing back and forth of frenzied Bookkeepers, nothing that reminded him of the world he had just risen out of, which now lay so far below him, like a bad dream. Then they were standing in a bright room whose walls were covered with red silk, with a large painting representing a nude woman, probably the famous Titian people were talking about, whose price was everywhere repeated in excited whispers. Delicate little pieces of furniture, a dainty desk, a small wall clock with silver pendulum, a gaming table surrounded by petite chairs, and flowers, roses, camellias, tulips, orchids, gladioli in spendthrift profusion, as though there were no seasons, no cold, no fog, and no winter. Almost as soon as they entered, a small side door opened and Petit-Paysan came in, dressed in a dinner jacket like the secretary, an India-paper edition of Hölderlin's poems in his left hand, index finger between the pages. The secretary withdrew. Archilochos and Petit-Paysan confronted one another.

"Well," Petit-Paysan said, "my dear Monsieur Anaximander . . ."

His name was Arnolph Archilochos, the Assistant Bookkeeper corrected him, bowing.

"Archilochos. Very good. I knew your name was something Greekish, Balkan, my dear Chief Bookkeeper."

"Assistant Bookkeeper." Archilochos set straight his social status.

"Assistant Bookkeeper, Chief Bookkeeper, it comes pretty much to the same thing, doesn't it?" the captain of industry said, smiling. "At least I don't make any distinction. How do you like my quarters up here? A lovely view, if I do say so myself. You can see the whole city, the river and even the Palace of the President, not to speak of the cathedral, and in the distance North Station."

"Very lovely, Monsieur Petit-Paysan."

"You are, incidentally, the first person from the Atomic Cannon Division to enter this floor," the industrialist said, as though congratulating Archilochos for performing an athletic feat.

"I am from the Obstetrical Forceps Division," Archilochos replied. "My territory is eastern Switzerland and the Tyrol, at present the canton of Appenzell Inner Rhoden."

"Well, well," Petit-Paysan exclaimed in surprise, "you come from the Obstetrical Forceps Division. I didn't know we made such things. What exactly are they?"

An obstetrical forceps, Archilochos explained, was an instrument used in childbirth. With it, the doctor grasped the baby's head during parturition, to speed delivery. The Petit-Paysan Engineering Works, Inc., manufactured forceps of various types; the differences lay in the shapes of the two fenestrated blades, which were curved to hold the head and also had a second curve known as the pelvic crook, to facilitate introduction of the instrument. The handles also varied; they might be short or long, of wood or metal, with or without special knobs and cross-grips; and furthermore there were distinctions in the type of hinge, that is, the arrangement which allowed the blades to open crosswise when in use. The prices . . .

"Why, you certainly know your subject," Petit-Paysan said smilingly. "But let's leave aside the question of price. Now, my dear Monsieur . . ."

"Archilochos."

"Archilochos, to make a long story short and not keep you in suspense any longer, I have appointed you Director of the Atomic Cannon. To be sure, you have just confessed that you belong to the Obstetrical Forceps Division, of whose existence I really had no inkling. That surprises me a little; something must have got mixed up somewhere; there are always mix-ups in a vast enterprise like this. Very well, it doesn't matter; let us simply combine the two divisions. Consider yourself hereafter Director of the Atomic Cannon and Obstetrical Forceps Division. I shall order the present Directors to be pensioned. I am happy to have the opportunity to inform you personally of your promotion, and to congratulate you."

"Director Zeus of the Obstetrical Forceps Division is already in the hospital."

"Why, what is his trouble?"

"Nervous breakdown."

"Goodness, then my intention must already have

reached him." Petit-Paysan shook his head in wonder. "And yet I only meant to dismiss Director Jehudi of the Atomic Cannon Division. Somehow there are always these leaks—too many loose tongues around. Well, good, Director Zeus has anticipated me with his nervous breakdown. I would have had to discharge him anyhow. Let us hope that Director Jehudi will receive the news with greater composure."

Archilochos pulled himself together, and for the first time ventured to look straight at Petit-Paysan, who still held the India-paper volume in his hand. "May I ask," he said, "what all this means? You send for me, promote me to the directorship of the Atomic Cannon and Obstetrical Forceps Division. I am disturbed because I must confess I do not understand any of this."

Petit-Paysan regarded the Assistant Bookkeeper calmly. He put the volume of Hölderlin down on the green gaming table, and with a gesture invited Archilochos to take a seat. They sat facing one another in the sunlight, on soft cushions. Archilochos scarcely dared breathe, so solemn was this moment. At last he would learn the reason for these mysterious events, he thought.

"Monsieur Petit-Paysan," he began anew, in a shy, halting voice, "I have always revered you. You are

Number Three in my ethical cosmos, the framework I have put together as best I could, in order to have a moral footing. You come immediately after our honored President and Bishop Moser of the Old New Presbyterian Church. I feel I should tell you all this. Hence I beg you all the more earnestly to explain the reason for your action to me. Bookkeeper Rummel and Chief Bookkeeper Petit-Pierre have tried to tell me that it is because of my reports on eastern Switzerland and the Tyrol, but I know nobody reads them."

"Dear Monsieur Agesilaus . . ." Petit-Paysan began solemnly.

"Archilochos."

"Dear Monsieur Archilochos, you were a Bookkeeper or Chief Bookkeeper—as I've said, I can't fathom the difference—and are now a Director. This seems to perplex you. Look here, my friend, you must see all these remarkable events in their worldwide connections, as a part of the highly diversified activities of my beloved Engineering Works. Why, the firm even—as I have just heard to my delight for the first time—manufactures obstetrical forceps. I hope this branch also turns a profit." Archilochos beamed. During the past three years, sixty-two obstetrical forceps had been sold in the canton of Appenzell Inner Rhoden alone, he reported.

"Hmm, not much of a turnover. But let that be. I suppose it is more or less a humanitarian division. Good to think that in addition to things that remove human beings from the world we also manufacture things that bring them into it. There must be a certain equilibrium, even if some products do not show a profit. So let us be grateful."

Petit-Paysan paused and looked grateful.

"In his poem 'Archipelagos,'" he continued at last with a bit of a sigh, "Hölderlin refers to the business man, the industrialist, as 'far-thinking.' The phrase has moved me deeply. A company like this is monstrous, my dear Monsieur Aristippus; the number of workmen and white-collar people, of Bookkeepers and stenographers, is vast, too vast to grasp. Why, I scarcely even know the Directors and have only a nodding acquaintance with the General Directors. The nearsighted go astray in this jungle. Only the man so farsighted that he does not keep his eye on details and individual destinies, but sees only the whole, will not lose sight of the distant goal, is far-thinking, as the poet puts it—you know his works, of course—only the man who knows how to dream, how to launch ever new enterprises, in India, in Turkey, in the Andes, in Canada—only such a man is not mired in the swamps of competition and cartels. Far-thinking. . . . I am on the point of making a merger with the Rubber and Lubricating Oil Cartel. That will be the coup of the century."

Petit-Paysan paused and looked far-thinking.

"So I plan, I work," he went on. "I add my few threads to the fabric being woven at the roaring loom of time. In my modest way, to be sure. What is the Petit-Paysan Engineering Works beside the Steel Trust or the Forever-Joyous Mines, the Pestalozzi Corporation or the Hösler-LaBiche! Nothing! But now, how does it stand with my employees? With all the individuals whose destinies I must overlook in order to keep my eye on the whole? This question frequently troubles me. Are they happy? World freedom is at stake; are my workers free? I have provided them with social benefits, with gymnasiums, swimming pools, canteens, vitamin pills, theatrical performances, concerts. But are the people to whom I give work still caught in material things, in filthy lucre? That is a question that haunts me. A Director goes to pieces merely because he is about to lose his job. Why, that's disgusting. How can anyone take money so seriously? Only the spirit counts, my dear Monsieur Artaxerxes; there is nothing more contemptible, more paltry than money."

Petit-Paysan paused once again and looked grave.

Archilochos scarcely dared stir.

But now the industrialist straightened up, stiffened; his voice rang out forcefully and coldly.

"You ask why I am appointing you Director. Very well, I shall give you the answer: In order not only to preach but to practice freedom. I do not know my employees, do not understand them; but evidently they have not yet fought through to a purely spiritual comprehension of the phenomenal world. Diogenes, Albert Schweitzer, St. Francis, do not seem to be their ideals, as they are mine. Apparently the members of the masses would forgo meditation, helpful service to others, the joys of poverty for the tinselly illusions of social status. Very well, let us give the world what it desires. I have always followed this rule of Lao-tse. For that very reason I have appointed you Director. So that justice may prevail in this regard also. The man who has risen from the ranks, who knows the cares and tribulations of employees from the very bottom, ought to be a Director. I plan the enterprise as a whole, but the man who deals with Bookkeepers and Chief Bookkeepers, with stenographers and secretaries, with errand boys and cleaning women, should be someone from their ranks. Director Zeus and Director Jehudi did not come from the ranks; I bought them as ready-made Directors from ruined rivals. Let us make an end to that. It is time for radical revision in our Western world. The politicians have failed. If industry should also fail, everything will go to the dogs, dear Monsieur Agamemnon. Man is wholly man only when he is creative. Your appointment represents a creative act, an act of creative socialism, which we *must* oppose to uncreative communism. That is all I have to say to you. From now on you are a Director—a General Director. But first take a vacation," he continued with a smile. "The cashier already has a check for you. Set yourself up. I saw you recently with a charming girl . . ."

"My fiancée, Monsieur Petit-Paysan."

"So you are about to marry. I congratulate you. Do so. Unfortunately, this happiness does not lie in my destiny. I have had a check for a General Director's annual salary made out to you. It will now be doubled, since you are also taking over the Obstetrical Forceps Division in addition to the Atomic Cannon Division— I have an important call to Santiago coming up—good luck, my dear Monsieur Anaxagoras. . . ."

As soon as

General Director Archilochos, once AB122-OF31, escorted to the elevator by the secretary, left the most holy precincts of the administrative building, he was received like a prince, was warmly embraced by General Directors, greeted with low bows by Directors. Stenographers cooed flatteringly around him, Chief Bookkeepers crept around the outskirts of the crowd, CB9-OF lurked in the background, dripping with servility, and from the Atomic Cannon Division, Director Jehudi was carried out on a stretcher, evidently in a straitjacket, exhausted and now unconscious. It was said that he had smashed all the furniture in his office. But it was the check that allured Archilochos, and he at once took possession of it. At least this is certain, he thought, still distrustful. He promoted CB9-OF to Vice Director of the Obstetrical Forceps Division, Numbers AB122-OF28, AB122-OF29, and AB122-OF30 to Bookkeepers, issued a few memos concerning the sales campaign for obstetrical forceps in the canton of Appenzell Inner Rhoden, and left the administrative building.

Now he sat in a taxi, for the first time in his life. Tired, hungry, bewildered by his precipitate rise in life, he had himself driven to Madame Bieler's.

The city lay in the grip of icy cold, under a clear sky. Everything looked abnormally distinct: palaces, churches, bridges; the big flag above the President's Palace seemed frozen stiff; the river was like a mirror; colors were stratified without blending; the shadows on streets and avenues had sharp outlines drawn around them.

Archilochos entered the bistro. The door tinkled as always, and he took off his shabby winter coat.

"Heavens above," Georgette said. She stood behind her counter, pouring herself a Campari, surrounded by bottles and glasses that sparkled in the cold sunlight. "Heavens above, Monsieur Arnolph! What's happened to you? You look pale and haggard, as though you've had no sleep, and turn up at a time when you should have been at the office long ago! Is anything wrong? Have you been to bed with a woman for the first time, or drunk wine? Have they gone and fired you?"

"On the contrary," Archilochos said, taking his corner seat.

Auguste brought him his milk.

"What does 'on the contrary' mean?" Georgette asked, perplexed. She lit a cigarette and puffed smoke into the slanting rays of sunlight.

"This morning I was appointed General Director of the Atomic Cannon and Obstetrical Forceps Division. By Petit-Paysan personally." Archilochos still spoke breathlessly.

Thereupon Auguste brought a bowl of applesauce, noodles, and salad to the table.

"Hmm," Georgette murmured. She did not seem overcome by the news. "Why?"

"As an act of creative socialism."

"Could be. And how did it go with the Greek girl yesterday?"

"We are engaged," Archilochos said shyly, blushing.

"That makes sense," Madame Bieler declared approvingly. "What sort of work does she do?"

"Housemaid."

"Funny sort of household she must work in," Auguste commented. "To afford a coat like that."

"Quiet!" said Georgette.

They had gone for a walk, Arnolph told them, and everything had been so strange, so odd, almost like a dream. All of a sudden everyone was greeting him, waving from cars and buses—the President, Bishop Moser, the painter Passap, and even the American Ambassador had called out "hello" to him.

"Aha," Georgette said.

"Maître Dutour also greeted me," Arnolph continued, "and Hercule Wagner, though he only winked."

"Only winked," Georgette repeated.

"Well, that kind," Auguste growled.

"Shut up!" Madame Bieler snapped at him, so violently that he skulked off behind the stove with his livid legs. "You don't have to put your oar in; this isn't anything a man could understand! So now you'll be able to marry your Chloé right away, I guess," she said, turning back to Archilochos and finishing her glass of Campari.

"I was thinking, as soon as possible."

"A good idea. It always pays to be decisive with women, especially when they're named Chloé. And where are you planning to live with your Greek wife?"

"I don't know," Archilochos sighed, as he buckled down to his applesauce and noodles. "My garret wouldn't do, of course, on account of the water closets and the bad air. In a boarding house, for the time being."

"Go on, Monsieur Archilochos, Georgette laughed.

"With the dough you're going to be making! Stay at the Ritz; that's where you belong. And from now on we're doubling your rates here. General Directors have to be exploited or they're no use to anyone."

She poured herself another Campari.

After Archilochos left, there was silence for a while in Chez Auguste. Madame Bieler washed glasses and her husband sat motionless behind the stove.

"That kind," Auguste said at last, rubbing his lean legs. "When I came in second in the Tour de France, I could have had one of that kind too, with a fur coat, fancy perfume, and an industrialist in tow—fellow who owned coal mines in Belgium. By now I'd probably be a General Director myself."

"Rot," Georgette said, drying her hands. "You weren't born for higher things. That kind of woman wouldn't marry you. There's nothing to wake up in you. Archilochos is a Sunday child—I've always felt that—and a Greek besides. You wait and see how he develops. He'll thaw out, and how! The woman is first-class. Only natural that she wants to get out of her trade. After all, it isn't always pleasant and it takes a lot out of you, in the long run. All of them want to get married; so did I. Of course the majority don't make it; they do end up in the gutter, as it always says in the sermons; some just about manage to land an Auguste with bare legs and a yellow bicycle rider's outfit—*eh bien,* I'm not complaining, if we're going to talk about bygone days, and I never had me an industrialist. I wasn't ever that classy. The only kind that came to me were petty bourgeois, a few boys from the Treasury, and once an aristocrat for two weeks, Count Dodo of Malchern, the last of his family. He's been dead and buried these many years. But that girl Chloé will pull it off. She has her Archilochos, and it's going to turn out pretty nice."

Meanwhile

Archilochos took a cab to the World Bank and then to a travel bureau on the Quai de l'État. He entered a big office with maps and bright posters on the walls. Visit Switzerland. The Sunny South Is for You. Air France to Rio. The Emerald Isle. Clerks with courteous, smooth faces. Rattle of typewriters. Neon lights. Foreigners speaking strange languages.

He wanted to go to Greece, Archilochos explained. To Corfu, the Peloponnesus, Athens.

"Sorry, our agency doesn't handle freighter travel," the clerk said.

But he wanted to go on the *Julia*, Archilochos explained. He would like to have a first-class stateroom for himself and his wife.

The clerk leafed through a timetable and gave a Spanish pimp (Don Ruiz) information on a train. "The *Julia* is booked up," he said at last, and turned to a businessman from Cairo.

Archilochos left the travel bureau and went back to his waiting taxi. He considered. Then he asked the driver who was the best tailor in the city.

The cab driver was surprised. "There's O'Neill-Papperer on the Avenue Bikini and Vatti on the rue St. Honoré," he replied.

"The best barber?"

"José on the Quai Offenbach."

"The best haberdasher?"

"Goschenbauer."

"Where does one buy the best gloves?"

"At De Stutz-Kalbermatten."

"Good," Archilochos said. "Take me to each of them in turn."

And so they drove to O'Neill-Papperer on the Avenue Bikini and to Vatti on the rue St. Honoré, to José on the Quai Offenbach, to De Stutz-Kalbermatten for gloves, and to Goschenbauer for hats. Archilochos passed through a thousand hands which smoothed, measured, cleaned, cut, massaged him; each time he entered the cab he was visibly changed, looking more suave and smelling more fragrant. After Goschenbauer's he wore a silver-gray Anthony Eden hat, and late in the afternoon he again drove up to the travel bureau on the Quai de l'État.

He wanted a first-class stateroom with twin beds on the *Julia,* he said in an unchanged voice to the clerk who had turned him away. He laid his silver-gray Anthony Eden hat on the glass counter.

The clerk began filling out a form. "The *Julia* sails next Friday," he said. "Corfu, the Peloponnesus, Athens, Rhodes, and Samos. May I have your name please?"

But after Arnolph had paid for the two bookings and left, the clerk turned to the Spanish pimp, who was still hanging around, leafing through travel folders and now and then conferring with various ladies who (likewise studying travel folders) slipped money into his thin, aristocratic hands.

"Scandalous, señor," the clerk said, practicing his night-school Spanish. "Some street cleaner or chimney sweep comes along and asks for two tickets on the *Julia,* which is really reserved only for the aristocracy and the best society" (he bowed to Don Ruiz). "Why, the passenger list for the next voyage includes the Prince of Hesse, and Mr. and Mrs. Weeman, and Sophia Loren. And when I head him off, out of pure kindness, because he'd find himself completely out of his element, the fellow comes back, sheer gall, dressed like a lord, rich as a tycoon, and I have no choice but to book a cabin for him—what can I do against capitalism? One of your cool customers who can make a fortune in three hours. Probably bank robbery, rape, murder, or politics."

"Simply outrageous," Don Ruiz replied in his night-school Spanish.

Darkness was beginning to fall and lights were going on in streets and houses when Archilochos drove across New Bridge to the Boulevard Künnecke and the residence of the Bishop of the Old New Presbyterians of the Penultimate Christians. But in front of the small Victorian house he found Bibi, ragged and dirty, with crushed hat, sitting on the curb, reeking of alcohol, his back propped against a lamp post, reading a newspaper he had found in the gutter.

"How come you're dressed up like that, Brother Arnolph?" he asked, whistling through his teeth, clucking his tongue, blowing his nose with his fingers, and carefully folding the filthy newspaper. "That's a pretty sharp outfit you've got on. Real high-class."

"I've become a General Director," Arnolph said.

"Well, I'll be damned."

"I'll give you a job as Bookkeeper in the Obstetrical Forceps Division if you promise to pull yourself together. Things have to be done right."

"No, Arnolph, I've got too much temperament for office work. Can you spare twenty centuries?"

"What's wrong now?"

"Gottlieb slipped down a building front and broke his arm."

"What building?"

"Petit-Paysan."

Archilochos became angry, for the first time in his life.

"Gottlieb has no business burgling Petit-Paysan's," he exclaimed. "He shouldn't be burgling at all. Petit-Paysan is my benefactor. As an act of creative socialism he has appointed me General Director, and now you ask me for money, money that comes to me from Petit-Paysan, after all."

"Won't happen again, Brother Arnolph," Bibi replied with dignity. "It was just practice. Gottlieb was a bit muddled. He'd heard there was a nice cache of Spanish gold at the Chilean Embassy; besides, the

Embassy building is easier to climb. He just mixed up the house numbers; after all, he's only a kid." He held out his fraternal palm. "Well, what about those centuries?"

"No," Archilochos said, "I cannot finance such dishonesty. I must see the Bishop now."

"I'll wait for you, Brother Arnolph," Bibi said, unabashed. He unfolded the newspaper again. "I have to study up on current events."

Bishop Moser,

stout and pink, in ministerial black and stiff white collar, received Archilochos in his study, a small, high-ceilinged, smoke-stained room lit only by a single lamp, with spiritual and secular books lining all the walls, a high window behind heavy drapes, through which fell the light of the lamp post under which Brother Bibi was ensconced.

The visitor introduced himself. He was actually an Assistant Bookkeeper, he said, but had just become General Director of the Atomic Cannon and Obstetrical Forceps Division in the Petit-Paysan Engineering Works.

Bishop Moser regarded him benevolently.

"I know, my good friend," he murmured. "You attend Preacher Thürcker's services at the Héloïse Chapel, don't you? I keep my eye on our dear Old New Presbyterian congregation. Welcome, welcome."

The Bishop vigorously shook the General Director's hand.

"Do sit down," he said, gesturing to a comfortable armchair and himself taking a seat behind his desk.

"Thank you," Archilochos said.

"Before you pour out your heart to me, I'd like to pour mine out to you," the Bishop murmured. "Will you have a cigar?"

"I am a non-smoker."

"A glass of wine? Brandy?"

"I am a teetotaler."

"Do you mind if I permit myself a cigar? A good Dannemann sets the mood for cozy talk and man-to-man confession. Sin bravely, Luther said. And I might say: Smoke bravely. And add: Drink bravely. Permit me?"

He filled a small glass with brandy which he kept in an old bottle behind some books.

"Oh, certainly," Archilochos said, somewhat perturbed. He was sorry that his Bishop was not quite the paragon he had always pictured.

Bishop Moser lit a Dannemann.

"You see, dear brother, as I hope I may call you, it has long been my heart's desire to have you in for a chat." (He puffed a first cloud of Dannemann smoke.) "But, dear God, you can't imagine how busy a bishop is. There are Old Age homes to visit, Youth Camps to organize, straying girls to find Christian homes for, the Sunday schools and confirmation instruction to be inspected, candidates to be examined, negotiations with the New Presbyterians to be conducted, our preachers to be given dressings down. There are a thousand things and trivia to take care of, and one never gets anything done. Our dear friend Thürcker has talked about you frequently; why, you never miss a single service and display a truly rare zeal for the work of our congregation."

His whole soul demanded that he attend services, Archilochos said simply.

Bishop Moser poured himself another pony of brandy.

"Exactly. We have all been most favorably impressed by you. Two months ago our Old New Presbyterian World Church Council lost one of its most venerable members and I have been considering whether you would not be the best candidate for this honorific post. It could certainly be combined with your duties as General Director—one would only have to play down the Atomic Cannon Division somewhat. But we need people who stand with both feet in the midst of the hard and often cruel struggle of life, Monsieur Archilochos."

"But Bishop Moser . . ."

"Well, are you willing?"

"It's an honor I'd never hoped . . ."

"Then may I propose you to the World Church Council?"

"If you think . . ."

"I would not want to conceal from you the fact that the World Church Council is receptive to my suggestions, often only too receptive. Only too often I live in the odor of tyranny; I have the reputation of being an overbearing Bishop of Bishops. They're all good-natured gentlemen and good Christians, to be sure— I'll say that for the World Church Council. They're grateful if I relieve them of organizational burdens and occasionally think for them—unfortunately not everyone has a bent for thinking, and that includes the World Church Council. The next World Council meeting is taking place in Sydney, Australia. After all, it's one of God's gifts to take a little trip like that, to get to know other countries and other peoples, foreign morals and foreign customs, the needs and problems of the common man the world over. Naturally the Old New Presbyterian Church pays the expenses."

"I am overcome."

"Well, that was my problem," the Bishop murmured. "Now let us come to yours. Speaking as man to man, sir. I can already guess it. You are considering marriage, contemplating linking your fortunes with a dear little woman. I saw you yesterday between the crematorium and the National Museum, and even greeted you, but I had to scurry down a depressing side street, there was a dying old woman I had to see, poor dear—another of God's hidden saints."

"Of course, Your Reverence."

"Well, have I guessed it?"

"Yes."

Bishop Moser closed the Greek Bible which lay on the desk before him.

"She was a pretty little thing," he said. "I congratulate you. When is the wedding to be?"

"Tomorrow. In the Héloïse Chapel, if possible— and I would be very happy if you could perform the ceremony."

The Bishop was somewhat embarrassed.

"That really is the job of your regular minister," he said. "Thürcker performs weddings splendidly; he has a remarkable sonorous voice."

"Won't you please make an exception?" Archilochos pleaded. "Since I'm going to be a World Church Councillor."

"Hmm. Do you think you can take care of the legal formalities so quickly?" the Bishop asked. Plainly, he was quite embarrassed about something.

"I shall ask Maître Dutour to take care of them."

The Bishop at last yielded. "Very well then. Shall we say tomorrow afternoon at three, in the Héloïse Chapel? May I have the name of your fiancée, address and so on?"

The Bishop noted down the necessary data.

"Your Reverence," Archilochos said, "my imminent marriage may be a sufficient reason for my taking up so much of your time, but it is not the prime reason, if I may say so, if it is not sinful to put it that way, since it would be difficult to find anything more important than entering on the obligation to live with a woman for a whole lifetime. Nevertheless, at this moment there is something far more important to me, something that lies heavily indeed upon my heart."

"My dear General Director, say all you wish to

say," the Bishop replied genially. "Courage. Cast the cares from your soul, whether your burden is a human or an all-too-human one."

"Your Reverence," Archilochos said timidly, straightening up in his easy chair and crossing his legs, "please forgive me if I seem to be talking confused nonsense. Only this morning I was dressed quite differently; I was frankly shabby, and the suit I wore was the one I'd worn at my confirmation. And now I suddenly find myself in expensive clothing made by O'Neill-Papperer and Vatti. I am distressed, Your Reverence; you must think I have succumbed completely to the world and its tinselly illusions, as Preacher Thürcker always says."

"On the contrary," the Bishop said, smiling. "An agreeable exterior, pleasing clothing, are entirely commendable, especially nowadays when it has become the mode in certain circles devoted to a Godless philosophy to dress with ostentatious carelessness, to look almost beggarly, with gaudy shirts hanging outside the trousers and similar outlandish attire. Decent nattiness and Christianity are by no means mutually exclusive."

"Your Reverence," Archilochos went on, encouraged, "it is a shock to a Christian, I think, when misfortune after misfortune suddenly descends upon him.

He may look upon himself as a Job who lost his goods and his health, his sons and his daughters; but for all that, he will be able to come to terms with the matter and regard his calamities as a consequence of his sins. But when the opposite happens, when one piece of good luck follows upon another, it seems to me the time has come for a man to be really disturbed. For where is there a human being who has deserved so much good fortune?"

"My dear Monsieur Archilochos," Bishop Moser said, smiling, "the nature of creation is such that this sort of case is extremely rare. The whole creation groaneth, as Paul says, and so we all groan under a greater or smaller accumulation of misfortunes, which, however, we should not take too tragically but understand more in the sense of Job, as you have so finely and correctly said, almost as eloquently as Preacher Thürcker. A case such as you have cited, such an accumulation of good fortune, is hardly likely to be found and produced anywhere."

"I am such a case," Archilochos said.

It was very quiet in the somber study. The last light of day was gone by now, blackest night reigned, and from the street scarcely a sound penetrated into the room, only the occasional hum of a passing automobile or the fading footsteps of a pedestrian.

"I have been struck by one piece of good fortune after the other," the former Assistant Bookkeeper continued softly. He sat there in his flawless suit, a chrysanthemum in his lapel (the silver-gray Eden hat, the immaculate white gloves, and the elegant fur coat were in the coat closet). "I inserted a notice among the matrimonials in *Le Soir*. The most charming girl imaginable answers my ad, loves me at first sight, and I love her at first sight; everything happens as in a cheap movie, so that I'm almost ashamed to talk about it. The whole city begins to greet me as I walk through the streets with this girl: the President, you, all sorts of important people; and today I've been accorded the most improbable sort of advancement both in the secular and in the ecclesiastical realm. I've been raised up out of nothing, from the miserable existence of an Assistant Bookkeeper to General Director and World Church Councillor. It's all inexplicable and deeply disturbs me."

For a long time the Bishop did not say a word. He suddenly looked old and gray, He stared into space, and had even laid the Dannemann in the ashtray, where it remained, abandoned and cold.

"Monsieur Archilochos," the Bishop said at last, abruptly ceasing to murmur and speaking in a different, firm voice, "all these events of which you tell me in private on this quiet evening are indeed strange and extraordinary. Whatever their underlying causes may be, I believe that these unknown causes" (here his voice trembled and for a moment dropped to a murmur again) "are not important to us, certainly not crucial, for they lie in the human realm, and in that realm we are all sinners. What is important, what all this means, is that you are a blessed person upon whom all the proofs of blessing are being heaped in their most visible manner. The man who must stand up before the world now is not Archilochos the Assistant Bookkeeper, but Archilochos the General Director and World Church Councillor. It must mean that you are now obligated to prove whether you deserve all these blessings. Take these events as humbly as you would if they were misfortunes; that is all I can think to tell you. Perhaps you are destined to tread an unusually difficult road, the road of good fortune, which is not imposed upon most people because they would understand even less how to tread it than the road of misfortune, which as a rule we have to traverse upon this earth. Good-by now." (He rose.) "We will see each other again tomorrow in the Héloïse Chapel. By then, perhaps, many mysteries will have been clarified for you, and I can only pray that you will not forget my words, no matter what befalls you henceforth."

After the conversation

with Bishop Moser in the smoke-stained, book-lined room with its sets of classics and rows of Bibles, its massive desk and heavy drapes, and after Bibi, still reading the newspaper (*Le Soir*) under the Bishop's window, had been paid off, the World Church Councillor would have liked to go straight to the Boulevard Saint-Père. But the clock on the Jesuit church at the Place Guillaume had only just struck six, and so he decided to wait until eight, as had been arranged, although he was painfully aware that this meant prolonging Chloé's life as a housemaid for two unnecessary hours. He resolved to move into the Ritz with her this very evening, and made the necessary arrangements, reserving two rooms, one on the second and one on the sixth floor, so that the girl should not feel awkward, and he himself, as a World Church Councillor, not be placed in a false position. Then he tried to locate Maître Dutour, but his efforts were unfortunately in vain. He was told that the lawyer and notary was out completing the transfer of title of a house. Even with all this, he still had more than an hour and a half to kill. He prepared himself, buying flowers and inquiring about a good restaurant. For he did not want to go back to his old temperance restaurant opposite the World Health Office; and Chez Auguste was not the right place either, for he felt with secret sorrow that his fine clothing excluded him from the bistro. An O'Neill-Papperer suit would not do alongside Monsieur Bieler's yellow jersey! He therefore decided, though with some twinges of conscience, to dine at the Ritz itself—a temperance meal, of course—and reserved a table. Then, atingle with happy anticipation, he went to the Passap show which he happened to notice at the Nadelör Gallery, just across the street from the Ritz; the attendance had been so large that the gallery was being kept open in the evening. Passap's latest paintings were on view (sixty-degree angles, ellipses, and parabolas). Archilochos, holding his flowers—white roses—moved slowly through the brightly lit rooms amid a throng of American women, journalists, and artists, enthusiastically and reverently studying the paintings. Suddenly he started at a canvas in cobalt blue and ocher which actually showed nothing but two ellipses and a parabola. Consulsively clutching his flowers, he stared in consternation at the painting. Then he suddenly whirled around, seized by deep dread, bathed in sweat and simultaneously shivering. He stopped for a moment at the cash register, where Nadelör, the gallery owner, stood in a black dinner jacket, smiling and rubbing his hands, and asked the painter's address. Then he dashed into a cab. The dealer, without bothering to take his coat, flew out the door after him and likewise jumped into a cab; he scented a secret purchase and was determined to make sure of his percentage. Passap lived on the Rue Funèbre in the Old Town. The cab (with Nadelor's close behind) finally reached the street by way of Marshall Vögeli Boulevard, but with considerable difficulty, for Fahrcks's followers were at the moment holding a demonstration, with pictures of the anarchist on long poles, red flags, and gigantic placards bearing such slogans as "Down with the President!" "Away with the Treaty of Lugano!" and so on. Somewhere in the mob Fahrcks himself was making a speech. Gales of shouting and screeching filled the air, whistles shrilled, horses' hooves thudded, and as the police began wielding nightsticks and fire hoses, the cabs containing the General Director and the art dealer were drenched. The latter had unfortunately opened a window, probably from curiosity. But then both vehicles with their swearing drivers turned into the Old

Town. The roughly paved streets rose steeply, lined with ramshackle houses and low dives. The whores stood around in swarms, like black birds, waving and uttering sharp, hissing sounds. It was so cold that the wet cabs became coated with ice.

At No. 43 on the ill-lighted rue Funèbre (where Passap lived), Archilochos got out, still holding the white roses. It was like stepping out of a fairy vehicle encrusted with sparkling, tinkling icicles. He told the cab driver to wait, and besieged by street urchins who clung to his trouser legs, he pressed on past a malignant, drunken concierge into the interior of the tall, ancient building. He began climbing endless flights of stairs which were so rotten that his foot broke through the steps several times and he hung for a moment in space, clinging to the banister. Wearily, he climbed from story to story, splinters in his aching hands, almost in darkness, peering at all the doors in search of Passap's name, hearing close behind him the panting of Nadelör, to whom he paid no attention. It was bitterly cold in the stairwell. Somewhere a piano tinkled and somewhere a window banged open and shut. Behind one door a woman was screeching and a man whooping; this landing smelled of wild orgies. Archilochos climbed higher and higher, once sinking through a step to his knee. He barged into a spider web; a fat, half-frozen spider ran across his forehead. Irritably, he brushed it aside. At last, Vatti's fur coat and O'Neill-Papperer's handsome suit covered with dust and his trousers already ripped, but with the flowers safe, he came to the end of a narrow, steep attic staircase and found a rickety door with Passap's name scrawled diagonally across it in gigantic chalked letters. He knocked. Two flights lower down, Nadelor waited in the icy cold. He knocked again, then a second, third, and fourth time. No one. World Church Councillor Archilochos pressed the latch. The door was unlocked, and he went in.

He found himself inside a vast attic, big as a barn. It was a tangle of beams, with various levels of flooring. Everywhere African idols stood around, piles of paintings, empty frames, sculptures, strangely twisted wire constructions, a glowing iron stove with a fantastically long, grotesquely winding stovepipe. Wine and whisky bottles lay about, squeezed-out tubes of pigment, cans of paint, brushes; cats were everywhere, and books lay piled on chairs and scattered on the floor. In the center of the room stood Passap in a once-white painter's smock, now splotched with color, dabbing away with his spatula at a canvas on the easel: parabolas and ellipses. Before him, close to the stove, a fat girl sat on a rickety chair, stark naked, with long blonde hair, hands clasped at the nape of her neck. The World Church Councillor stood petrified, scarcely daring to breathe; this was the first time he had ever seen a naked woman.

"Who the devil are you?" Passap asked.

Archilochos introduced himself, though he was rather surprised at the question, for the painter had greeted him on Sunday.

"What do you want?"

"You painted my fiancée, Chloé, naked," the Greek choked out.

"You mean the painting *Venus, July 11,* which is now hanging in the Nadelör Gallery."

"Exactly."

"Get dressed," Passap snarled at the model, who vanished behind a screen. Pipe in mouth, its smoke curling up among the tangle of beams, Passap stood looking long and attentively at Archilochos.

"So what?"

"Sir," Archilochos replied with the utmost dignity, "I am an admirer of your genius. I have followed your career with rapt interest, have even elevated you to the rank of Number Four in my cosmos."

"Your cosmos? What nonsense is this?" Passap asked, heaping fresh mounds of paint (cobalt blue and ocher) on his palette.

"I have drawn up a list of the worthiest representatives of our age, a list of my moral exemplars."

"Well?"

"Sir, in spite of the enthusiasm I feel for your work, in spite of my deep respect, I must ask you for an explanation. It is certainly not an everyday occurrence for a bridegroom to see his bride depicted naked as Venus. And even though the painting is an abstraction, a sensitive observer cannot fail to recognize the subject."

"Pretty damn good," Passap said. "More than the critics can do."

He studied Archilochos once more, stepped up to him, felt him over like a horse, took several steps back again, and squinted at him.

"Undress," he said then. He poured himself a glass of whisky and filled a fresh pipe.

"But . . ." Arnolph attempted to protest.

"No buts," Passap snarled at him, his small black eyes so fierce and piercing that Archilochos fell silent. "I want to paint you as Ares."

"Ares?"

"The war god of the Greeks," Passap explained. "I have been searching for years for a suitable model, for the pendant to my Venus. You are it. The typical raging lion, lover of the heat of battle, organizer of blood-baths. You are Greek?"

"Certainly, but . . ."

"There you are."

"Monsieur Passap," Archilochos said at last, "you are mistaken. I am no raging lion, neither an organizer of bloodbaths nor a lover of the heat of battle. I am a peace-loving man, World Church Councillor of the Old New Presbyterian Church, a strict teetotaler, and I also refrain from smoking. Moreover, I am a vegetarian."

"Nonsense," Passap said. "What is your occupation?"

"General Director of the Atomic Cannon Division and the . . ."

"There we have it," Passap interrupted. "A war god after all. And a raging lion. You are simply repressed and have not yet arrived at the mode of life which is appropriate for you. You are also a born swiller and lecher, the most magnificent Ares that has ever come my way. So get undressed and be quick about it. My business is painting, not gabbing."

"Not while this woman you were painting is still in the room," Archilochos protested.

"Scram, Catherine, he's bashful," the painter

shouted. "I won't need you again till tomorrow, fatty."

The fat, blonde-haired girl, now with her clothes on, departed. As she opened the door, she confronted Nadelör, covered with ice, shaking in every limb from cold.

"I must protest," the art dealer called out hoarsely. "I must protest, Monsieur Passap. We agreed . . ."

"Go to the devil!"

"I'm trembling in every limb from cold," the art dealer cried desperately. "We agreed . . ."

"Freeze to death."

The girl shut the door. She could be heard clumping down the stairs.

"Well," the painter impatiently asked Archilochos, "aren't you out of your pants yet?"

"All right," the General Director replied, undressing. "My shirt, too?"

"Everything."

"The flowers? They're for my fiancée, you see."

"Put them on the floor."

The World Church Councillor laid his clothes neatly over a chair, brushed them out with his hand (for they were covered with dust from the laborious climb up the stairs), and at last stood naked.

He shivered with cold.

"Move the chair over to the stove."

"But."

"Stand on the chair and take a boxer's pose, arms at angles of sixty degrees," Passap ordered. "That is how I have always imagined a war god."

The chair teetered on its rickety legs, but Archilochos obeyed.

"You're too fat," the painter growled irritably, pouring himself another glass of whisky. "I only go for that in certain women. But I can get around it. The main thing is the face and chest. All that hair on your chest is good, has a martial look. And the thighs are all right. But take those glasses off; they spoil the whole illusion for me."

Then he began to paint, angles of sixty degrees, ellipses, and parabolas.

"Sir," the World Church Councillor began anew (in his boxer's pose), "you owe me an explanation . . ."

"Shut up!" Passap thundered. "If there's to be any talking here, I'll do it. It's the most natural thing in the world that I painted your fiancée. A magnificent woman. You'll find that out when you get to know her breasts."

"Sir . . ."

"And her thighs, her navel."

"But I must . . ."

"Get back into a decent boxer's pose, damnitall," the painter snarled, smearing wads of ocher on the canvas, followed by cobalt blue. "Why, you don't even know your girl nude and yet you risk an engagement."

"You're stepping on my flowers. White roses."

"So what. A revelation, that nude. I had to force myself not to become a banal naturalist or a bright-buoyant-bouncy-beatific impressionist when I saw that glorious flesh, that breathing skin. Pull your belly in, damnitall! I never had a more divine model than Chloé with her divine back, those perfect shoulders, and those two rounded buttocks, like the twin halves of the universe. A sight like that puts cosmic ideas into your mind. Painting became a pleasure such as it hadn't been for ages. Ordinarily I don't much care for women as subjects—only now and then, like that fat one I had here. Artistically they don't yield anything special. A man is different; there the deviations from the classic ideal are precisely the interesting feature. But with Chloé now—that was different! In her you still see the unity of Paradise—her legs, her arms, her neck, grow out of her body with perfect naturalness, and her head is still a woman's head. I've also done a sculpture of her. Here!"

He pointed to a structure of tangled wires.

"But . . ."

"Boxer's pose," Passap admonished; he stepped back several times, examined his painting, changed an ellipse, removed the canvas from the easel, and screwed a fresh one into place.

"There," he commanded. "Now kneel. Ares after the heat of battle. Lean forward more; after all, I don't have you available every day."

Archilochos, confused and half roasted by the stove, put up only a feeble resistance.

"I would really like to ask you . . ." he said, but was interrupted by Nadelör, who came tottering, shaking in every limb, into the attic, a moving, tinkling lump of ice, convinced that a sale was being negotiated.

Passap flew into a rage.

"Clear out!" he cried, and the art dealer crept back into the arctic cold of the stairwell.

"Art is my explanation," the painter said at last, drinking whisky, painting, and simultaneously caressing the tomcat which had climbed on his shoulders. "I don't give a damn whether or not this explanation satisfies you. I have made something out of your nude fiancée, a masterpiece in proportions, in distribution of planes and rhythms, in color, in painterly poetry—a world of cobalt blue and ocher. You, on the other hand, want to make something entirely different out of Chloé, once you have her at your disposal in the nude.

A mama with a flock of kids, I guess. You will destroy a masterpiece of Creation, sir, not I, who glorify this masterpiece, raise it to the realm of the Absolute, the Ultimate, the dream."

"It's a quarter after eight," Archilochos exclaimed in alarm, although at the same time he felt relieved by the painter's explanation.

"So what?"

"I'm supposed to meet Chloé at eight," Arnolph explained anxiously. Cats purring around his legs, he started to step down from his chair. "She's waiting for me at the Boulevard Saint-Père."

"Let her wait. Keep your pose!" Passap roared. "Art is more important than your love affair." He went on painting.

Archilochos groaned. The cat, a gray one with white paws, had now climbed to his shoulders, and its claws dug painfully into his flesh.

"Quiet," Passap ordered. "Don't move."

"The cat."

"There's nothing wrong with the cat, but there is with you," the painter said angrily. "How can anyone develop such an enormous belly, and without drinking, too?"

Nadelör once more appeared at the door (numb, coated with ice). He was frozen through, he sniveled, his voice so hoarse as to be almost inaudible.

"Nobody's asked you to wait outside my door, and I don't want you in my studio," Passap retorted roughly.

"You do business with me," the art dealer croaked; he had to sneeze but could not get his hand out of his pocket because his sleeve was frozen to his trousers.

"On the contrary, you do business with me," the painter thundered. "Get out!"

The art dealer withdrew for a third time.

Archilochos did not dare say another word. Passap drank whisky, painted angles of sixty degrees, parabolas and ellipses, heaped cobalt on ocher and ocher on cobalt, and after half an hour allowed the General Director to dress.

"Here," Passap said, putting the wire construction in his arms, "Put this beside your marital bed. My wedding present. So that you will remember your wife's beauty when it fades. And I'll send you one of your portraits after it dries. And now get out. I dislike World Church Councillors and General Directors almost as much as I do art dealers. Your luck that you look like the Greek god of war. Otherwise I would have thrown you out long ago, naked, believe me!"

Archilochos departed,

the white roses in one arm, while the other clasped the wire construction which allegedly represented his naked fiancée. On the steep, narrow stairway, which was really rather a ladder, he encountered Nadelör. Icicles had now formed under the art dealer's nose. He stood huddled next to the wall, utterly miserable and frozen through from the icy draft.

"There you are," the man lamented, his voice as faint as if it were coming from a crevice in a glacier. "I thought so. You've bought something. I protest."

"It's a wedding gift," Arnolph explained. He began cautiously descending the stairs, hampered by the flowers and his wire sculpture, vexed with himself at his senseless adventure, for it was going on nine o'clock. But the condition of the stairs did not allow any more rapid descent.

The art dealer followed him.

"You ought to be ashamed," Nadelör grumbled, to the extent that his words were at all comprehensible. "I heard you telling Passap that you're a World

Church Councillor. Scandalous. A high churchman acting as a model! Stark naked!"

"Would you please hold the sculpture for me?" Archilochos was forced to ask him after a time (between the fourth and third floors, near the still screeching woman and whooping man). "Just for a moment; my foot has gone through the step."

"Impossible," Nadelör whispered. "I never touch a sculpture unless I get my percentage."

"Then hold the flowers."

"I can't. My sleeves are frozen hard."

At last they reached the street. The icicled cab gleamed like silver. Only the radiator was free of ice, and the motor was still running. Inside, it was frigid. The heater was out of order, the shivering driver explained.

"Twelve Boulevard Saint-Père," Archilochos said, his spirits reviving at the prospect of seeing his fiancée shortly.

The cab was just about to start when the art dealer tapped on the windowpane.

"I must ask you to give me a lift," came indistinctly from the mass of ice as Arnolph lowered the window and leaned toward the glittering blob. He managed to make out the art dealer's plaint that he could not go a step further and that taxis were few and far between in the Old Town.

"Impossible," Archilochos said. "I must get to the Boulevard Saint-Père. I'm already terribly late."

"You're a Christian and a World Church Councillor," Nadelör replied accusingly. "You can't leave me in this condition. I'm already beginning to freeze to the sidewalk."

"Get in," Archilochos said, flinging open the cab door.

"A bit warmer in here anyhow, it seems to me," the art dealer said when he at last managed to bend himself and sit beside Archilochos. "I hope I thaw out."

But by the time they turned into the Boulevard Saint-Père, Nadelör had not yet thawed. Nevertheless, he also had to leave the cab. The driver refused to go back to the Quai. He'd had enough of the cold, he said, and off he drove. So the two stood before the wrought-iron gate with its putti and dolphins, with the red lamp, which was now dark, and two stone pillars. Archilochos pulled at the old-fashioned bellpull. No one answered. The boulevard was deserted. In the distance the noise and shouts of the demonstrating followers of Fahrcks could be heard.

"Sir," Archilochos said, upset by his lateness, the

flowers and wire sculpture in his arms, "I must leave you now."

Resolutely he opened the gate; but Nadelör followed him into the depths of the garden.

"What do you want now?" Arnolph asked, vexed that he could not get rid of the ice-coated art dealer.

"I must telephone a cab."

"I hardly know the people here . . ."

"You as a World Church Councillor . . ."

"All right, all right," Archilochos said. "Come along."

The cold was merciless. The art dealer rang like a glockenspiel as he walked. The fir and elm trees stood motionless; huge stars twinkled in the sky, reddish and yellowish amid the silvery ribbon of the Milky Way. Among the tree trunks the windows of a villa glowed in muted gold. As they came closer they saw that the building was really a small rococo palace, daintily ornate, with slender columns, the whole bedecked with vines of wild grape, which showed up plainly on this clear night. A gently curving staircase led up to the front door, which was brightly lit and without a nameplate. Beside it hung a heavy bellpull, but once again no one answered the ring.

Another minute in this cold and he would be frozen to death, the art dealer wailed.

Archilochos pressed the latch. The door was unlocked. He would go and see, he said.

Nadelör entered with him.

"Are you crazy?" demanded Archilochos.

"I can't stand outside in this cold . . ."

"I'm not at home here."

"You as a Christian . . ."

"Then wait here," Arnolph ordered him.

They had entered a large salon. Furniture which
reminded Archilochos of Petit-Paysan's quarters,
flowers and little mirrors, beneficent warmth everywhere. The art dealer began thawing immediately.
Little streams of water ran down him.

"Don't stand on the rug," the World Church Councillor snapped, but he felt somewhat alarmed for the
gallery owner at the sight of all the drip.

"Certainly," Nadelör said, posting himself beside
the umbrella stand. "If only I may use the phone."

"I'll ask the master of the house."

"As soon as possible."

"At least hold the wire sculpture," Archilochos suggested.

"Only for a percentage."

Arnolph placed the work of art beside Nadelör and
opened a door. He looked into a small salon with a
settee, a small tea table, a spinet, and delicate little

armchairs. He cleared his throat. The room was empty, but he heard footsteps behind a double door. Evidently Mr. Weeman. He crossed the room, knocked.

"Come in!"

To his astonishment Arnolph found himself confronting Maître Dutour.

Maître Dutour,

a small, spry man with a black mustache and an artistic mop of white hair, stood at a large, handsome table in a room walled with golden mirrors. A chandelier full of real candles hung from the ceiling, brilliant as a Christmas tree.

"I have been expecting you, Monsieur Archilochos," Maître Dutour said, bowing. "May I ask you to take a seat."

He indicated a chair, and sat down facing the World Church Councillor. A document was spread out on the table.

"I don't understand," Archilochos said.

"My dear General Director," the lawyer said, smiling, "I have the pleasure of transferring this house to you as a gift. It is free of mortgage and in excellent condition, except for the west side of the roof, which ought to be repaired one of these days."

"I still don't understand," Archilochos said. Though surprised, he was already somewhat inured to so much good fortune. He was in the way of it, after all. "Would you mind explaining . . ."

"The former owner of the house does not wish his name mentioned."

Oh, he knew who that was, Arnolph declared. The owner was Mr. Weeman, the famous archaeologist and excavator of Greek antiquities, who'd dug up some ancient temple with precious statues buried in a bog, and golden columns.

Maître Dutour started, stared wonderingly at Archilochos, and shook his head. He was not permitted to dispense any information, he said; the previous owner wished to have his house in Greek hands, and was happy to have found in Archilochos a man who met these conditions. In an age of corruption and immorality, he continued, an age in which the most unnatural crimes seemed to be the most natural, in which all right-thinking was on its way out and people were turning individually and collectively to the fist-and-club morality of primitive eras, a man of law would lose all hope of ever seeing any meaning in his efforts for order and justice if he were not privileged now and then to prepare and execute an act of pure *caritas* such as the transfer of this mansion. The documents were all ready; the General Director had only to glance through them and sign his name. The tax required by the government—Moloch demanded his victims—had already been paid.

"Thank you very much," Archilochos said.

Maître Dutour read the documents aloud, and the World Church Councillor signed his name in the proper places.

"This little palace now belongs to you," the lawyer said, rising.

Archilochos likewise rose. "Sir," he said solemnly, "let me express my pleasure at meeting a man whom I have always revered. You were the defense attorney for that poor curate. It was a case of the flesh overpowering the spirit, you cried out at the time; the soul remained untainted. Those words made a deep impression upon me."

"Now, now," Dutour said, "I was only doing my duty. Unfortunately the curate was beheaded; I still feel bad about it. I plumped for twelve years in the penitentiary, you know. Though at least I was able to avert the worst: the poor fellow was not hanged."

I I I

"May I trouble you for a moment longer?" Archilochos said.

Dutour bowed.

"I wish to ask you, *cher Maître,* to prepare the papers for my marriage."

"They are prepared," the lawyer replied. "Your dear fiancée has already asked me to."

"Oh," Arnolph exclaimed joyfully, "you know my dear fiancée?"

"I have had the pleasure."

"Isn't she a wonderful girl?"

"Very."

"I am the happiest man in the world."

"Whom do you suggest as witnesses?"

He had not yet thought about it, Archilochos admitted.

"I would recommend the American Ambassador and the Rector of the University," Dutour proposed.

Arnolph hesitated.

"I have already won their consent," Maître Dutour said. "It will not be necessary for you to do anything further. The marriage is already creating a sensation in society—word of your amazing career has got around, my dear Monsieur Archilochos."

"But these gentlemen do not know my bride."

The little lawyer threw back his mop of hair,

stroked his mustache, and contemplated Arnolph with an almost spiteful stare.

"Oh, I fancy they do," he said.

"I understand." It suddenly dawned on Archilochos. "The gentlemen have been guests of Gilbert and Elizabeth Weeman."

Again Maître Dutour started and seemed surprised. "So to speak," he said finally.

Arnolph was not altogether enthusiastic. "Of course I have great esteem for the Rector of the University..."

"There you are."

"But the American Ambassador . . ."

"Do you have political objections?"

"Not that," Archilochos replied falteringly. "Mr. Forster-Monroe does after all take fifth place in my moral cosmos; but he belongs to the Old Presbyterian Church, whose dogma of Universal Reconciliation I cannot share, for I believe unshakably in the eternity of hellfire."

Maître Dutour shook his head. "I don't want to say anything against your religion," he said. "But surely all that's beside the point. There should not be much in common between the eternity of hellfire and your marriage."

Archilochos sighed with relief. "I quite agree with that," he said.

Maître Dutour closed his briefcase. "I will bid you good-by now," he said. "The civil ceremony will take place at two o'clock at City Hall."

Arnolph wanted to see him to the door.

He would rather go across the garden, the lawyer said. He pushed aside a red drape and opened a tall casement. "This is the shortest way."

Icy air streamed into the room.

He must have been a frequent guest here, Archilochos thought as the lawyer's swift footsteps faded into the night. For a few moments Arnolph stood on the terrace outside the glass door. He gazed at the twinkling stars above the trees. Then, shivering, he stepped back into the room and closed the casement. "The Weemans must have entertained a great deal," he murmured.

Archilochos

began wandering through the little rococo palace which now belonged to him. It had seemed to him that he heard faint footsteps in an adjoining room, but he found no one. The whole house was illuminated, either by big white candles or by small lamps. He passed through parlors and small sitting rooms, filled with graceful, delicate furniture, the floors covered with soft rugs. On the walls hung precious antique wallpapers, sometimes rather frayed, with pale-gold lilies against a silver-gray background and fine oil paintings which, however, he did not dare to look straight at; rather, Archilochos blushed several times, for most of them showed nude women, occasionally joined by men equally in a state of nature. He found Chloé nowhere.

At first he had wandered about planlessly, but after a while he began following a colored trail, paper cutouts of blue, red, and golden stars which lay on the soft rugs and seemed obviously meant to guide him. He came at last to an unexpected narrow, winding staircase which he reached through a secret door in the wallpaper, and so climbed to the upper floor (he had stood baffled for a long time in front of the wall where the stars ended, until at last he discovered the door). On every step lay either a paper star or a paper comet, and once the planet Saturn with its ring, then the moon, then the sun. From step to step Archilochos grew more and more irresolute; his courage had fled and his old timidity had overcome him. He breathed heavily, clutching the white roses which he had never let out of his hand, even during the conversation with Maître Dutour. The winding staircase ended in a round room with a large desk and three high windows, a globe of the world, a high-backed chair, a big standing lamp, and a chest—all the furniture had a medieval cast, as in Faust's study in the theater. A sheet of yellowed parchment lay on the chair. On it was written in lipstick: ARNOLPH'S STUDY. At the sight of the telephone on the desk, Archilochos thought for a moment of the waiting gallery owner standing dripping beside the umbrella stand in the hall down below —perhaps he had thawed out completely by now. But he forgot Nadelör by the time he opened the other study door, to which the stars and comets led; for now he saw before him a bedroom with a tremendous, antique canopied bed. ARNOLPH'S BEDROOM was inscribed on the sheet of parchment which lay on a small Renaissance table. The next room—he continued following the track of stars—switched back to rococo; it was a charming boudoir lit by little red lamps, with all the fragile objects and furniture appropriate to such a room. CHLOÉ'S BOUDOIR was written here, and the lipsticked parchment lay on a chair over which some articles of clothing had been tossed in hasty disorder— clothing that befuddled Archilochos: a brassière, a girdle, a slip, panties, all gleaming white. On the floor lay stockings and shoes, and through a half-opened door he looked into a black-tiled bathroom. The tub, set into the floor, was filled with green scented water, slightly steaming; but the comets on the floor pointed not only to the bathroom but through it to another door, which he thereupon opened, holding the flowers before him like a shield. He entered a bedchamber with a delicately carved but extremely wide canopied bed in the center. Here the stars and moons ended, except for a few pasted to the footboard; but there was no one to be seen, for the curtains of the bed were drawn. A few logs burned in a fireplace, casting Arnolph's shadow, huge and flickering, upon the red bed curtains, which were embroidered with strange golden devices. Timidly, he approached the bed. Peering through the crack between the curtains, he saw in the darkness nothing but the white cloud of bed linen. But it seemed to him that he could hear breathing, and so he whispered softly, gripped by a thousand anxieties: "Chloé." No one answered. He had to act, much though he would have preferred to retreat, from the room, from the palace, back to his garret where he was safe and not befuddled by stars. And so at last with heavy heart he drew the curtain aside and found her lying there, her head ringed by the black tendrils of her loosened hair, sleeping.

Archilochos was so dazed that he sagged down on the edge of the bed and looked shyly at Chloé. But he only dared to look now and again. He was tired, too; the unceasing good fortune had never given him a chance to rest and reflect; so that his shadow on the filmy vermilion curtain of the canopied bed drooped closer and closer to the sleeping Chloé. But suddenly he observed that Chloé had opened her eyes slightly and was studying him, had probably been doing so for some time, from under her long lashes.

"Oh," she said, as if awakening, "Arnolph. Did you find the way all right, through all those rooms?"

"Chloé," he exclaimed, startled, "you're lying in Mrs. Weeman's bed."

"The bed belongs to you now, you know," she laughed, stretching.

"You told Mr. and Mrs. Weeman about our engagement, didn't you?"

She hesitated. "Of course," she said after a moment.

"Whereupon they gave us this little palace."

"They have several more in England."

"I don't know," he said, "I can't really take it all in yet. I had no idea Englishmen were so socially enlightened and would simply make their maid a present of a palace."

"It seems to be the custom there in certain families," Chloé explained.

Archilochos shook his head. "And I have become General Director of the Atomic Cannon and Obstetrical Forceps Division."

"I know."

"At a huge salary."

"So much the better."

"And also World Church Councillor. In May I must make a trip to Sydney."

"That can be our wedding trip."

"No," he said, "this!" He took the two tickets from his pocket. "We're sailing to Greece on Friday. On the *Julia*."

But then he gave a start.

"How is it you know all about my career?" he asked.

She sat up, and was so beautiful that Archilochos lowered his eyes. She seemed about to say something, but then abandoned it, with a sigh, looked long and pensively at Arnolph, and sank back into the pillows. "The whole city is talking about it," she said at last, in an odd voice.

"And tomorrow you want to marry me," he stammered.

"Don't you want to marry me?"

Archilochos still did not dare to look, for she had thrown aside her blanket. Altogether, it was difficult to look anywhere in this room; everywhere were pictures of naked goddesses and gods, something he would not have expected of flat-chested Mrs. Weeman.

"These Englishwomen," he thought. "Fortunately they are good to their maids, so one can forgive them their lewd minds." What he really wanted to do was to lie down, take Chloé into his arms, and simply sleep, for hours, dreamlessly and soundly in the warm glow of the fireplace.

"Chloé," he said softly, "everything that has happened is so confusing to me, and probably to you also, that sometimes I scarcely feel like myself any more and I think I've turned into someone else and must really still be in my garret with its mildewed walls, and that you have never existed. It's much harder to endure happiness than unhappiness, Bishop Moser said today, and at times I think he is right. Unhappiness is not surprising; it happens because it's in the nature of things; but happiness occurs by accident, and so I'm full of fear that our happiness will end as quickly as it began, and that everything is a game people are playing with you and me, with a housemaid and an Assistant Bookkeeper."

"You mustn't brood about all this now, darling,"

Chloé said. "I've waited for you all day, and now you're here. And how handsome you are. Won't you take off your coat? It's certainly made by O'Neill-Papperer."

But as he started to take it off, he realized that he still held the flowers in his hands.

"Here," he said, "white roses."

He wanted to give her the flowers, and had to lean across the bed, but was embraced by two soft white arms and drawn down on to it.

"Chloé," he gasped, "I haven't yet explained to you the fundamental dogmas of the Old New Presbyterian Church." But at this moment someone cleared his throat behind him.

The World Church Councillor

started up, and Chloé hid under the blanket with a cry. It was the gallery owner who stood beside the canopied bed, shivering, teeth rattling, wet as a drowned man just pulled out of the water, hair pasted to his forehead in thin strands, mustache dripping, clothes plastered to his body, Passap's wire sculpture in his hands. From his feet all the way to the door stretched a puddle, glistening in the candlelight, a few paper stars floating in it.

"I've thawed out," the art dealer said.

Archilochos stared at him.

"I've brought the sculpture."

"What do you want?" Arnolph asked at last, blushing.

"I didn't mean to intrude," Nadelör replied, shaking his sleeves, from which water was running to the floor as if they were hoses. "But I must ask you as a Christian and a World Church Councillor to please telephone a doctor at once. I've a terrible fever, stabbing pains in my chest, and a ghastly backache."

"All right," Arnolph said, rearranging his clothing and standing up. "Perhaps you'd better put the sculpture right here."

"As you wish," Nadelör replied. Groaning, he placed the sculpture beside the bed. "I also have inflammation of the bladder."

"My fiancée," Archilochos made the introduction, gesturing to the mound formed by the blanket.

"You ought to be ashamed," the art dealer said, fresh fountains spurting from him. "You as a Christian . . ."

"She really is my fiancée."

"You may count on my discretion."

"Will you please go now," Archilochos said, propelling Nadelör out of the room; but in the boudoir the gallery owner stopped again beside the chair bearing the brassière, the girdle, and the panties.

A bath would do him good, he said, gesturing with trembling arm toward the open bathroom door and the steaming green water in the sunken tub.

"Impossible."

"You as a World Church Councillor . . ."

"As you like," Archilochos replied.

Nadelör undressed and stepped into the bath.

"Don't go away," he begged, naked in the bathtub, soft-fleshed, drenched in sweat, his eyes large, pleading, and feverish. "I might faint."

Then Archilochos had to massage him.

The gallery owner showed signs of anxiety.

"What if the master of the house should turn up?" he quavered.

"I am the master of the house."

"But you said . . ."

"The house has just been turned over to me."

The man had a high fever and his teeth were chattering. "Owner or not," he said, "no one is going to turn me out of this place in my condition."

"It is true, I assure you," Archilochos said. "Trust me."

He still had a little common sense left, Nadelör gasped, heaving himself out of the tub. "You as a Christian. I'm terribly disillusioned. You're no better than all the others."

Archilochos wrapped him in a blue-striped bathrobe that hung in the bathroom.

"Take me to a bed now," the art dealer groaned.

"But . . ."

"You as a World Church Councillor . . ."

"All right."

Archilochos led him to the canopied bed in the Renaissance room. He tucked him in. "I'll telephone the doctor now," Adolph said.

"First a bottle of cognac," the gallery owner demanded, shivering, his throat rattling. "I always take it for colds. You as a Christian . . ."

"I'll look in the cellar," Archilochos promised, and wearily started to descend the stairs.

But as soon as he reached
the cellar stairs, after some wandering about, he heard
a distant whooping from below. Everything was lit up,
moreover, and when he reached the vaulted wine cellar
he found his presentiment confirmed: Brother Bibi
was sprawling on the floor, with the twins Jean-
Christophe and Jean-Daniel, in the midst of emptied
bottles, singing folksongs.

"Behold what cometh from on high!" Bibi cried
cordially when he caught sight of his brother. "Uncle
Arnolph!"

What was he doing here? Arnolph asked anxiously.

"Digging out the brandy and practicing harmony.
Who'll go a-hunting? said Robin to Bob . . ."

"Bibi," Arnolph said with dignity, "I should like to
ask you not to sing. This is the cellar of my house."

"Well, well," said Bibi, "you have come up in the
world. Congratulations. Plank yourself down here,
Brother Arnolph, square on the sofa." He offered his
brother an empty keg that stood in a puddle of red
wine.

"Come on, kids," he urged the twins, who were doing gymnastics, like monkeys, on Arnolph's knee and shoulders, "Rap out a hymn for your uncle."

"Be faithful, honest, true, and good . . ." Jean-Christophe and Jean-Daniel sang screechingly.

Archilochos attempted to overcome his weariness. "Brother Bibi," he said, "I have to talk to you once and for all."

"Enough with the music, twins!" Bibi bumbled thickly. "Listen sharp. Uncle Arnolph wants to make a speech."

"Not that I am ashamed of you," Arnolph said. "You are my brother and I know that at the bottom of your heart you're a good soul, who bears no man ill-will, with inner nobility. But because of your weakness I must now be stern as a father with you. I have supported you, and the more I gave you, the worse things have gone with you and your family. And now here you are lying drunk in my cellar."

"Sheer oversight, Brother Arnolph; I thought it was the War Minister's cellar. Just an oversight."

"So much the worse," Arnolph replied sadly. "One does not break into strangers' cellars. You'll end up in prison. Now go home with your twins, and tomorrow you'll start work at Petit-Paysan in the Obstetrical Forceps Division."

"Home? In this cold?" Bibi demanded, horrified.

"I'll call a cab for you."

"You want my delicate twins to freeze to death?" Bibi protested indignantly. "In our drafty barracks they'd die in this temperature. It's four below zero."

From an adjoining section of the cellar came rumbling sounds. Matthew and Sebastian, twelve and nine years old, rushed in, dashed at their uncle, and joined the twins in clambering on his knees and shoulders.

"Put away your daggers when you play with your uncle, Matthew and Sebastian," Brother Bibi commanded.

"Good Lord," Arnolph asked from underneath his four nephews, "who else have you got here?"

"Only Mama and Uncle Captain," Bibi said, opening a bottle of vodka. "And then just Magda-Maria with her new sport."

"The Englishman?"

"What's this about an Englishman?" Bibi said in a tone of wonderment. "That was all over with long ago. A Chinese now."

When he finally returned to Nadelör, the man was asleep, though tossing with delirious dreams, and it was too late to telephone a doctor. Archilochos was exhausted. Cacophonous sounds of singing still came from the cellar. He did not dare follow the trail of stars and comets a second time to Chloé's bedroom. Instead, he lay down on the settee, near the chair with the brassière and girdle, and after removing his O'Neill-Papperer coat at last and covering himself with it, fell asleep at once.

In the morning

he was awakened toward eight o'clock by a maid in a white apron.

"Hurry, sir," this maid said, "take your coat and leave, before the master of the house wakes up." She opened a door which he had not noticed previously and which led out to a wide hallway.

"Nonsense," Archilochos said, "I am the master of the house. The man in bed is the gallery owner Nadelör."

"Oh," the girl said, dropping a curtsy.

"What is your name?" he asked.

"Sophie."

"How old are you?"

"Sixteen, sir."

"Have you been here long?"

"Six months."

"Mrs. Weeman hired you?"

"Mademoiselle Chloé, monsieur."

Archilochos thought there must be some confusion somewhere, but he felt uneasy and forbore to ask any further questions.

"Would you like your coffee, sir?" the girl asked.

"Is Mademoiselle Chloé up yet?"

"She sleeps till nine."

"Then I wish to see her at nine," Archilochos said.

"*Mon Dieu,* monsieur!" Sophie shook her head. "Then Mademoiselle takes her bath."

"And at half past nine?"

"She is massaged."

"Ten?"

"Monsieur Spahtz comes."

"Who is that?" Archilochos asked.

"The dressmaker."

"But when can I see my bride?" Archilochos cried out in despair.

"*Ah non,*" Sophie declared firmly. "There are all the wedding preparations. Mademoiselle has far too much to do."

Archilochos submitted and told the girl to show him

to the breakfast room; at least he would have something to eat.

He breakfasted in the room in which Maître Dutour had transferred the house to him, served by a stately, gray-haired butler (the whole place seemed suddenly to be swarming with servants). Eggs, ham (which he let stand), mocha, orange juice, grapes, and sweet rolls with butter and jam. Outside the tall windows, meanwhile, it grew lighter beyond the trees of the garden, and the wedding presents began pouring into the palace. Flowers, letters, telegrams, mountains of packages. Blowing their horns, the mail trucks drove up, became jammed one behind the other; the presents were heaped higher and higher in the hall, in the salon, even in front of the bed and on the blanket of the forgotten art dealer, who with mute dignity went on with his delirium.

Archilochos wiped his mouth with the damask napkin. He had eaten for almost an hour, conscientiously, silently, for since his noodles and applesauce at Georgette's he had not had so much as a morsel. On the sideboard stood bottles of apéritifs and liqueurs, boxes of cigars, brittle, fragrant Partagas, Dannemann, Costa Penna, a fine array of cigarettes. The first temptation to try something of the sort arose in him; alarmed, he fought down the feeling. He was enjoying this first hour as master of the house. To be sure, the singing and bawling of Bibi's clan, which at times sounded only too clearly from the cellar, bothered him somewhat. The fat cook, who had gone down there, came back badly disheveled; she had almost been raped by Uncle Captain.

A band of robbers had broken in, the alarmed butler reported, and wanted to telephone the police. Archilochos waved that aside.

"Just my family."

The butler bowed.

Arnolph asked his name.

"Tom."

"Age?"

"Seventy-five, sir."

"How long have you been here?"

"Ten years."

"Mr. Weeman hired you?"

"Mademoiselle Chloé."

Again Archilochos thought there must be some confusion, but for the second time forbore to pursue his questioning. He felt slightly uneasy before this seventy-five-year-old butler.

O'Neill-Papperer would be coming at nine o'clock, the butler informed him. To prepare the wedding suit. Goschenbauer had already sent the top hat.

"Very good."

"At ten the registrar. There are still a few formalities to settle."

"Very well."

"At half past ten Monsieur Wagner will call to bring the honorary doctorate of the Medical Faculty of the University, for Monsieur's services in connection with obstetrical forceps."

"I shall be expecting him."

"At eleven the American Ambassador is coming with a letter of congratulations from the President of the United States."

"Delighted."

"At one there will be a small lunch with the witnesses and at twenty minutes to two departure for the Registry Office. After the ceremony in the Héloïse Chapel, dinner at the Ritz."

Who had organized all this? Archilochos wanted to know.

"Mademoiselle Chloé."

"How many guests?"

Mademoiselle desired an intimate celebration. Only close friends.

"I entirely agree."

"Therefore we have invited only two hundred persons."

Archilochos was somewhat perplexed. "Very well," he said at last. I don't understand these matters. Have a cab here for me at half past eleven."

"Wouldn't you prefer Robert to drive you?"

"Who is that?" Archilochos asked.

"The chauffeur. Your red Studebaker is the smartest in the city, sir."

"Odd," Archilochos thought; but at this moment O'Neill-Papperer arrived.

And so, shortly before half past eleven, he drove to the Ritz to call on Mr. and Mrs. Weeman. He found the two in the hotel lobby, a feudal room with plush sofas and all sorts of armchairs, with such dark paintings on the walls that the objects represented, various fruits in some and assorted game in others, were all but invisible. The couple were sitting on a sofa, reading magazines: he the *New Archaeological Survey* and she the *Journal of Antiquities*.

"Mr. and Mrs. Weeman," Arnolph addressed them, stirred to his depths, handing them two orchids as they looked up in surprise, "you are the finest persons I have ever known."

"Well," Mr. Weeman said, pulling on his pipe and laying aside the *New Archaeological Survey*.

"I am raising you to Numbers One and Two in my ethical cosmos!"

"Yes," Mr. Weeman said.

"I revere you even more than the President and the Bishop of the Old New Presbyterians."

"Well," said Mr. Weeman.

"Who gives from the heart deserves thanks from the heart."

"Yes," said Mr. Weeman, staring popeyed at his wife.

"Thank you very much!"

"Well," said Mr. Weeman, and then again, "Yes." He took out his wallet, but Archilochos had already vanished.

"Dear good people, but rather reserved, these Englishmen," he thought as he rode away in his red Studebaker (the smartest in the city).

It was not just a few meek little old ladies of the Old New Presbyterian congregation that awaited the wedding procession in front of the Héloïse Chapel. Huge crowds of people stood half frozen on Emil Kappeler Street and formed long rows along the sidewalks. Every window of the dirty, battered quarter was filled with heads and shoulders. Ragged urchins hung like lime-sprayed grapes from the lampposts and perched in the neighborhood's few wretched trees. The procession of automobiles turned from the Boulevard Merkling, on its way from City Hall to the Chapel, the red Studebaker in the van. Chloé and Archilochos emerged from the Studebaker. The crowd screamed and roared with enthusiasm. "Hurrah for Archilochos!" *"Evviva Chloé!"* The bicycle-racing fans shouted themselves hoarse, and Madame Bieler and her Auguste (for once not in his cyclist's outfit) both wept. Somewhat later the President's ornate carriage came driving up, drawn by the six white horses, the bodyguard with golden helmets and white plumes on prancing black chargers. The Héloïse Chapel filled. It was not exactly a beautiful building, since it rather resembled a small factory, had no tower, and it's once-white walls were badly marred. It was, in fact, in every respect an unsuccessful product of modern ecclesiastical architecture, surrounded by a few dreary cypresses. And since it had once taken over for a song the furnishings of an extremely old church which had had to be demolished to make room for a movie palace, the interior of the Héloïse Chapel corresponded to its exterior. It had a barren, poverty-stricken air, with crude wooden benches and a rude pulpit which projected, awkward and solitary, into the room. Opposite the entrance was a large, half-rotted cross. The wall behind the cross, with its yellow and greenish stains, reminded Archilochos of his former garret, as did the high windows, like loopholes; through them fell slanting rays of light in which danced particles of dust. But as the wedding guests began to occupy this poor, devout, cramped world, which smelled of old women, of cheap perfume, and perhaps also of garlic, brilliance entered; the chapel became friendly and warm; the sparkle of jewelry and pearl necklaces filled the room; shoulders and breasts glowed, and fumes of the finest perfume rose upward into the half-charred rafters (the church had once nearly burned down). Bishop Moser mounted the pulpit, dignified in his black Old New Presbyterian robe. He laid the Bible with its bright gilt edging on the cracked wood of the lectern, clasped his hands, and looked down, somewhat embarrassed, it seemed, his pink face drenched with sweat. Directly below him sat the bridal couple, Chloé with big, black, fervent eyes, radiant with joy, in a filmy veil in which played a ray of sunlight, and Archilochos stiffly at her side, now also embarrassed, in his formal dress (O'Neill-Papperer), hardly recognizable any more, for only his rimless, dusty glasses, which were now somewhat askew, remained of his old self. The top hat (Goschen-bauer) and the white gloves (De Stutz-Kalbermatten) rested on his knees. Behind the pair, but somewhat apart from the others, sat the President, goateed, his face chiseled by innumerable lines, hair white, his uniform of a cavalry general bedizened with gold, long sword along his thin legs, on which he wore highly polished boots; and behind the President sat the witnesses: the American Ambassador, with decorations on the breast of his white formal jacket, and the Rector magnificus in all his gravity; then came the guests, rather uncomfortably seated on the wooden benches: Petit-Paysan; Maître Dutour at the side of his enormous wife, who towered into the room like a mountain covered with pearls instead of snow; Passap, he too in tails, his hands still stained with cobalt blue; in addition, men, chiefly men, of the upper one thousand, the cream of the cream of the city, all solemn-faced; and just as the Bishop was about to begin his oration even Fahrcks came in, though late: Fahrcks the revolutionary, the last and lowermost in Arnolph's ethical cosmos, huge, massive head with bristly mustache and fiery red, curly hair between mighty shoulders, double chin touching the breast of his tailcoat, from which dangled a gold decoration studded with rubies: the Order of the Kremlin.

Bishop Moser

began his address in a low, faintly lisping voice, shifting back and forth in his pulpit with visible discomfort. The words of which he wished to remind the congregation assembled here to celebrate this happy occasion, he said, were to be found in the Seventy-second Psalm, a Psalm of Solomon: Blessed be the Lord, the God of Israel, who alone does wondrous things. His task today, the Bishop continued, was to bind together for life two children who undoubtedly had been dear and precious to all those gathered here in the Héloïse Chapel. There was first of all the bride (here Bishop Moser stammered a little), whom all those present had no doubt locked in their hearts with great tenderness, a bride who (here Bishop Moser became poetic) had so graciously vouchsafed to all those assembled here so much love, so much of beauty and sublimity, in brief so many glorious hours, that no one could thank her sufficiently (the Bishop wiped the sweat from his brow); and here was a bridegroom, the Bishop continued with manifest relief, also a dear, noble soul who would now partake of all the love which his bride was capable of giving so lavishly—a citizen of our town who in a few days had attracted the attention of the whole world, rising from humble estate to the eminence of General Director, World Church Councillor, Honorary Doctor of the Medical Faculty, and Honorary Consul of the United States. True though it might be that everything man undertakes, and all that he achieves, all his titles and deserts, are transitory, chaff in the wind, a nothingness in the face of the Eternal, nevertheless this precipitate rise showed that grace had intervened (here Fahrcks audibly cleared his throat). For all this was simply not a grace bestowed by men alone (now Petit-Paysan cleared his throat), but by God, as the Scriptural passage just quoted indicated; not the favor of men had elevated Archilochos, but the Lord alone, who to be sure had employed for His purposes human hearts which He guided, had indeed utilized human weakness, human fallibility, for His ends, and therefore to Him alone belonged the glory.

So Bishop Moser preached, and his voice grew more powerful, more stirring, his words more elaborate, more unctuous, the further he moved from the starting point of his oratory, the bride and bridegroom, to the realms of the infinite and the divine,

painting a canvas of the wisely and majestically ordered cosmos in which the decrees of God ultimately
turned all things to a good end. But after the Bishop
had finished, and had descended from the pulpit and
completed the ceremony, the two whispering their "I
do's," and Archilochos now stood there, his lovely
wife, with her big, black, happy eyes, holding his arm,
and as if awakening, he looked at the fine company
through which he was now to pass, the dignified President, the ladies and gentlemen weighed down with
jewelry and decorations, all these powerful, influen-
tial, and famous persons in the land, and as he noticed
Fahrcks with his tousle of red hair scrutinizing him
mockingly, face twisted in a malignant grimace, and
as the little organ above the choir began wheezing out
Mendelssohn's Wedding March—at this point, at the
climax of his joy, envied by the waiting crowd outside,
the Greek suddenly understood. He paled, reeled.
Sweat poured down his face.

"I HAVE MARRIED A COURTESAN!" he cried
out desperately, like a fatally wounded animal. He
wrenched away from his wife, who anxiously pursued
him in her waving veil to the portal, and ran out of the
Héloïse Chapel, where the crowd received him with
whoops and gales of laughter, for as they saw the

bridegroom appear alone they instantly realized what had happened. Archilochos faltered for a moment among the miserable cypresses, alarmed, for only now did he realize the vast numbers of the spectators. Then he ran past the President's carriage and the waiting line of Rolls-Royces and Buicks and dashed down Emil Kappeler Street, zigzagging because here and there people stepped in his way. He ran frantically like a hunted animal pursued by a pack of dogs.

"Hurrah for the town cuckold!"

"Down with him!"

"Tear his clothes off!"

Whistles shrilled in his ear, insulting shouts and stones were hurled after him, urchins tripped him up. Several times he fell, until finally, covered with blood, he was able to hide under the stairs in the entrance to a tenement house. He cowered there in the darkness, the thundering footsteps of the pack above his head, his face buried in his arms. After a while the pursuit stopped, since the mob had lost its quarry.

For hours he continued to crouch under the stairs, freezing, sobbing softly, while it grew darker and darker in the unheated hallway of the tenement. She had slept with all of them, all, with the President, with

Passap and Maître Dutour, with all of them, he whimpered. The whole enormous weight of his moral cosmos had collapsed, crushing him in the ruins.

Finally he pulled himself to his feet. He staggered down the unknown hallway, fell over a bicycle, and stepped out on the street. Night had already fallen. He stole down to the river, through ill-lighted, dirty streets, stirring up hordes of yammering beggars who lay under the bridges wrapped in newspapers. A dog snapped at him, shadowy in the darkness. Squeaking rats scurried past and gurgling water lapped at his feet. Somewhere, a ship's whistle howled.

"That's the third one this week," a beggar's voice squawked. "Go on, jump in!"

"Nonsense," another croaked. "It's too cold."

Laughter.

"Hang yourself, hang yourself," the beggars bawled in chorus. "That's the easiest, that's the easiest."

He left the river, wandering at random through the Old Town. Somewhere the Salvation Army was playing a hymn. He drifted into the Rue Funèbre, where Passap lived, began to run, trudged for hours through quarters he had never entered before, through high-toned residential streets, working-class neighborhoods filled with the noise of radios, past ugly taverns from which boomed the cynical songs of Fahrcks's adherents, through factory districts with ghostly foundries, and toward midnight reached his old garret. He did not turn on the light; he stood leaning against the door which he had closed behind him, trembling, filthy, O'Neill-Papperer's dress suit torn; he had long ago lost Goschenbauer's top hat. The flushing toilets still roared, and the lights from the little windows in the building across the areaway fell through the dusty windowpanes, illuminating now the curtain (behind which hung his old Sunday suit), now the iron cot, now the chair and the rickety table with the Bible, now the pictures of his former cosmos against the vague wallpaper. He opened the window. Stench welled up toward him, and a louder roaring. One after the other he ripped the pictures from the wall, hurled the President, the Bishop, the American Ambassador, even the Bible, into the dark depths of the shaftlike areaway. He left hanging only Brother Bibi with his little brood. Then he crept into the other part of the attic, where long rows of laundry hung indistinctly, untied a clothesline, left the wash of some family or other lying on the floor, and groped his way back to his rom. He placed the table under the lamp, climbed up on it, fastened the clothesline to the hook from which the lamp hung. Then he knotted the noose. The window blew open and shut, and icy drafts washed across his forehead. He stood, head in the noose, and was about to throw himself from the table when the door to his room opened and the light was turned on.

It was Fahrcks, still in formal dress as at the wedding, a fur-lined coat over it, his ponderous face immobile, gigantic above the Order of the Kremlin, his tousle of hair a furious flame. Two men accompanied him. One of them was Petit-Paysan's secretary, who now bolted the door, while the other, a towering hulk of a man in the uniform of a taxicab driver, closed the window. Then, chewing gum, he placed the chair in front of the door. Archilochos stood on the swaying table, head in the noose, in the spectral light of the lamp. Fahrcks sat down on the chair and folded his arms. The secretary sat down on the bed. The three remained silent. With the window closed, the roar of flushing toilets was somewhat muted, and the anarchist sat studying the Greek closely.

"Well, Monsieur Archilochos," he said at last, "you really should have expected me to call."

"You too have slept with Chloé," Archilochos snarled at him from his stance on the table.

"Of course," Fahrcks said. "After all, that is the lovely lady's occupation."

"Get out!"

The revolutionary did not stir. "Each of her lovers gave you a wedding present," he said. "Now it's my turn. Luginbühl, hand him my present."

The giant in cab driver's uniform stepped to the table, chewing, and laid a metallic, egg-shaped object between Arnolph's feet.

"What is that?"

"Justice."

"A hand grenade?"

Fahrcks laughed. "Exactly."

Archilochos took his head out of the noose, climbed carefully down from the rickety table, and hesitantly picked up the grenade. It was cold and sparkled in the light.

"What am I supposed to do with it?"

The revolutionary did not answer at once. Immobile, cunning, he leaned forward on the chair, huge hands spread out over his knees.

"You wanted to commit suicide," he said. "Why?"

Archilochos did not answer.

"There are two ways to deal with this world," Fahrcks said slowly and dryly. "Either one is destroyed by it or one changes it."

"Be still," Archilochos screamed.

"Very well. Then hang yourself."

"Say your say."

Fahrcks laughed. "Give me a cigarette, Schubert," he said, turning to Petit-Paysan's secretary. Luginbühl gave him a light from a clumsy lighter, and he sat smoking deliberately, puffing out big, bluish clouds of smoke.

"What am I to do?" Archilochos cried.

"Accept what I am offering you."

"What for?"

"The social order that has made a fool of you must be overthrown."

"That's impossible."

"Nothing is easier," Fahrcks replied. "You are to assassinate the President. I'll take care of the rest myself." He tapped the Order of the Kremlin.

Archilochos reeled.

"Don't drop the bomb," the old incendiary warned him. "It will explode if you do."

"You want me to become a murderer?"

"What's so awful about that? Schubert, show him the plan."

Petit-Paysan's secretary stepped to the table and unfolded a sheet of paper.

"You're in league with Petit-Paysan!" Archilochos cried out, horrified.

"Nonsense," Fahrcks said. "I've just bribed the secretary. Such fellows can be had for small change."

Here was the plan of the President's palace, the secretary began explaining matter-of-factly, running his finger over the drawing. Here the wall surrounded the palace on three sides. The front side was closed off by an iron fence thirteen feet high. The wall itself was seven feet nine inches high. To the left was the building of the Economics Ministry, to the right the Nuncio's residence. Where the wall enclosed the courtyard of the Economics Ministry, a ladder was standing.

Archilochos wanted to know whether the ladder was always there.

"It is there tonight; that ought to be enough for you," the secretary replied. "We will drive you as far as the Quai. You climb up the wall, draw the ladder after you, and use it to climb down. On the other side you will be in the shade of a fir tree. Step behind the trunk of it and wait until the guard has passed. Then proceed along the back of the palace. You will find a small door, with several steps leading up to it. The door is locked; here is the key."

"And then?"

"The President's bedroom is on the second floor; from the little door you reach it by way of the main staircase. It is toward the rear. Throw the hand grenade at his bed."

The secretary fell silent.

"And after I have thrown the grenade?"

"Go back the way you came," the secretary said. "The guards will all be rushing through the main entrance and you will have time to escape across the courtyard of the Economics Ministry, in front of which our car will be waiting for you."

It was silent in the garret, and cold. Even the roar of water closets had ceased. Against the stained wallpaper Brother Bibi and his little brood hung in solitude.

"Well?" Fahrcks interrupted the silence. "What do you say to this project?"

"No," Archilochos cried, pale, shaking with horror. "No!"

The old revolutionary dropped his cigarette to the rough floor (splintery wood with big knotholes), where it went on smoldering.

"They all take on like that at first," he said. "As though the world could be changed without killing."

Next door, awakened by Arnolph's cry, a servant girl thumped on the wall. Archilochos saw himself, Chloé on his arm, walking through the wintry city. Fog hung over the river with its big, shadowy ships and its lights. He saw people waving from streetcars, from automobiles, handsome, elegant young men. Then he saw the wedding guests, spangled with gold and studded with diamonds, black tailcoats and evening dresses, scarlet decorations, white faces in the golden sunlight, with the dancing dust particles, and everyone wearing a benevolent smile that was in truth so false, so malicious. He felt once again the sudden, cruel moment of insight, of shame; saw himself rushing out of the Héloïse Chapel, emerging from among the cypresses; saw himself faltering, and at last beginning his wild dash down Emil Kappeler Street, right through the howling, jeering, jubilant crowd. He saw the shadows of his pursuers grow to gigantic size on the asphalt of the street, felt once again his body pitching forward, felt the impact of his fall on the hard ground, which reddened with blood, and the stones, the fists that struck him like hammers, and how he quivered as he crouched under the stairs of the hallway, with footsteps pounding above him.

"I'll do it," he said.

Archilochos,

resolved to avenge himself upon the world, was driven by Fahrcks and his companions in their American-made car to the Quai Tassigni. From here he had only two minutes' walk to the President's palace on the Quai de l'État. It was fifteen after two. The Quai was deserted. A quarter moon had risen behind St. Luke's Cathedral. The ice floes in the river, and the bizarre crenellations and beards on the frozen St. Cecilia's Fountain, glistened in its light. Archilochos kept in the shadow of the palace and the hotel. He passed by the Ritz with its shivering doorman who paced up and down in front of the entrance; but otherwise he met no one. Only Fahrcks's car drove by several times, as if by chance; the revolutionary was checking to see that Archilochos carried out his mission. Fahrcks also stopped to ask the policeman in front of the Economics Ministry some feigned question, so that Archilochos could slip unnoticed into the courtyard. There he found the ladder against the wall. He patted the grenade in the pocket of his patched old coat, which he had taken with him from the garret, climbed the ladder, sat down on the narrow top of the wall and drew it after him, dropped it to the other side and descended. When he reached the hard-frozen lawn, he found himself in the shadow of a fir tree, just as the secretary had said. Arc lights were playing on the side of the building toward the Quai, and an automobile blew its horn somewhere; perhaps that was Fahrcks again. The quarter moon emerged from behind the Presidential Palace, a clumsy, over-ornamented baroque structure (reproduced in all art books and extolled by all art commentators). Close to the moon a big star twinkled, and the lights of an airplane moved high up in the sky. Then footsteps resounded on the paved path that wound along outside the palace. Archilochos pressed close to the trunk of the fir, hidden in its branches, which hung down to the ground and surrounded him with their resinous scent, while the needles tickled his face. There were two guards; they approached marching in step, visible at first only as dark silhouettes with shouldered rifles and fixed bayonets, their white plumes swaying in the moonlight. In front of the fir tree, they came to a halt. One of them pushed the branches aside with his rifle. The Greek held his breath, thought himself discovered, and was already preparing to throw the grenade. But then they moved on; they had not seen him. As they advanced into the full moonlight, their golden helmets and the cuirasses of their historical uniforms flashed brightly. They turned the corner of the palace. Archilochos disentangled himself from the branches of the tree and sprinted toward the rear of the building. There everything lay in the full glare of the moonlight: tall spruces and bare weeping willows, an ice-coated pond and the Nuncio's residence. He found the door at once. The key fitted. He turned the key, but the door did not open. It must be bolted from inside. Archilochos hesitated; the guards might be back at any moment. He stepped back and looked up the rear wall of the building. The door was embedded between two nude marble giants, evidently Castor and Pollux, who carried a curving balcony on their shoulders. The balcony, he deduced, must be outside the President's bedroom. A mad fury of determination seized him: he must carry out the assassination, come what may. He began scaling one of the statues, clambering up a thigh, a belly, a chest, digging his fingers into a marble beard, holding on to a marble ear, hoisting himself up over a gigantic head. He reached the balcony. In vain. The door would not open, and he did not dare smash the glass panes, for he could already hear the guards' footsteps. He flattened himself out on the cold floor of the balcony. The guards came along, marching in step as before, and passed by beneath him. The balcony door was surrounded by a variety of nude males and females, larger than life, with horses' heads among them, all brightly illuminated by the moon, fighting and rending one another in gruesomely complex postures. He was able to study all this while still lying on the floor of the balcony. Evidently it represented a battle with Amazons, and in the midst of the writhing bodies he detected the open hole of a round window. He ventured up into the world of marble gods, made his way between enormous breasts and thighs, fearing all the while that the bomb in his coat pocket might explode. He crawled past the bellies of heroes, along arched and twisted backs, at one point had only the drawn sword of a warrior to hang on to, snatching at it just as he thought he had already fallen. Terrified, he thrust himself into the arms of a dying Amazon whose sophisticated face beamed tenderness upon him, while far below the guards completed their tour for the third time, and stood still.

Archilochos saw them step back into the moonlit gardens and study the wall of the palace.

"There's someone up there," one of the two said, after prolonged peering.

"Where?" the other asked.

"There."

"Nonsense, that's only a shadow between the gods."

"They aren't gods, they're Amazons."

"What's that?"

"Women with only one breast."

"But they've got two."

"The sculptor made a mistake," the first guard concluded. "But someone's hanging on up there. I'll bring him down fast enough."

He raised his rifle and took aim. Archilochos did not move.

The other man protested: "Do you want to wake the whole neighborhood with your target practice?"

"But there's someone there."

"There isn't. No one could ever get up there."

"Guess you're right."

"You see? Let's go!"

The two marched off, in step, their rifles shouldered again. Arnolph clambered on, at last reached the window, and crawled through it. He found himself on the third floor, in a high-ceilinged bare toilet, filled with moonlight that streamed through the open window. He was exhausted, covered with dust and bird droppings from his climb, and sobered by the abrupt change between the world of marble gods and his present place. Breathing heavily, he opened the door and found himself in a spacious hall which opened up on both sides into large rooms of state, they too moonlit, with statues among the columns. Vaguely, he made out a wide, curving staircase. He descended cautiously to the second floor, reached the corridor the secretary had described, peered through the tall windows on the side toward the Quai, and started back in alarm, momentarily blinded by the lights of the city. In the yard below the guard was being relieved: a solemn ceremony with salutes, clicking heels, standing at attention, and goose-stepping. He glided back into the darkness, crept toward the bedroom door at the farther end of the corridor, and opened it softly, hand grenade in his right hand. Through the tall balcony door fell quivering moonlight; that was the door he had stood in front of when he was outside. He entered the room, looking for the bed, prepared to throw the hand grenade; but there was no bed in the room, no sleeping President, only a basket with dishware. Otherwise the room was empty. He had been wrongly informed. Anarchists, too, must go astray sometimes. Confused, he withdrew, and began stubbornly searching for his victim. He went up to the third floor again, the bomb held ready, then to the fourth, wandering through sumptuous reception rooms, conference rooms, corridors, small parlors, entering offices with covered typewriters, picture galleries, a weapons room with ancient armor, cannon, and banners, where a halberd ripped his sleeve. At last, when he climbed to the fifth floor and was stealing cautiously along the marble wall, he saw a crack of light ahead. Someone must have turned on a light. He summoned up his courage and walked on. The hand grenade gave him a sense of power. He entered the corridor. His weariness had vanished. He looked down the corridor, which ended at a door. It was ajar. In the room, a light was burning. He hurried over the soft rug; but when he wrenched open the door, hand with the grenade raised, the President stood before him in his bathrobe. The sight was so sudden and surprising that Archilochos barely had time to conceal the grenade in his coat pocket.

"I beg your pardon,"

the assassin stammered.

"Ah, there you are, my dear Monsieur Archilochos," the President exclaimed joyfully, grasping the confused Greek's hand and shaking it vigorously. "I've been expecting you all evening, and a while ago I happened to see you from my window, climbing over the wall. A good idea. My bodyguard is far too pedantic. The fellows would never have admitted you. But now you're here, and I'm so delighted. How ever did you get into the building? I was just about to send my valet down. I've been living on the fifth floor only for the past week; it's much more comfortable here than on the second, although there is the difficulty that the elevator doesn't always work."

The back door had been unlocked, Archilochos stammered; he felt that he had missed the right moment, and besides he was standing too close to his victim.

"How fortunate," the President said warmly. "My valet, old Ludwig—he really looks much more like a President than I do—has rustled up a little supper."

"I beg your pardon," Archilochos said, flushing. "I didn't mean to intrude."

"Not at all, not at all," the goateed old man assured him. "At my age one doesn't sleep much—cold feet, rheumatism, worries, personal and public, what with the present tendency of nations to collapse, and so I often have a bite to eat during the long nights in my lonely palace. Luckily we had central heating installed last year."

"It really is pleasantly warm," Archilochos observed.

"Why, what a sight you are!" the President said. "Covered with dust. Ludwig, brush him off a little."

"Permit me," the valet said, and began cleaning the dust and bird droppings off the assassin's clothing. Archilochos did not dare to fend him off, though he was afraid the bomb in his coat pocket might explode as a result of the brushing. He was relieved when the valet helped him out of his coat.

"You resemble my butler at the Boulevard Saint-Père," he said.

"As a matter of fact he is my half-brother," the valet replied. "Twenty years my junior."

"We have a great deal to chat about, I imagine," the President said, leading his would-be murderer down the now brightly illuminated corridor.

They entered a small room on the Quai side of the building, lit by candles. In a window embrasure stood a small table set with precious china and sparkling crystal on a white linen cloth.

"I'll strangle him," Archilochos thought surlily. "That's the simplest way."

"Let us sit down, my dear good friend," the courteous old President said, lightly touching Arnolph's arm. "From here we can gaze down into the yard if we like, at those upstanding young men with their white plumes who would be surprised to learn that someone has made his way in to me. The idea of the ladder is excellent, and delights me all the more because I too sometimes climb over the wall by means of a ladder, in the dead of night, as you have just done—but that is between the two of us. An old President must sometimes employ such means, for there are aspects of life that concern a man of honor but not the gentlemen of the press. Ludwig, pour us the champagne."

"Thank you," Archilochos said. "But I'll kill him nevertheless," he thought.

"And a bit of chicken," the old man said with unconcealed pleasure. "Ludwig and I always have that in the kitchen, champagne and chicken at three o'clock in the morning. Good, simple fare. I assume your climb over the wall has made you good and hungry."

"Rather," Archilochos said honestly, thinking of his climb up the face of the building. The valet served them with perfect dignity, although his hands trembled in an alarming manner.

"Don't be upset by Ludwig's shaking," the President said. "He has already served six of my predecessors."

Arnolph cleaned his glasses with the napkin. The grenade would have been more convenient, he thought. He did not yet know how he would go about it. He could not very well say, "Excuse me," and begin strangling the President. Besides, the valet would have to be done away with, lest he call the guards. And so Archilochos ate and drank, in the first place in order to gain time and adjust to the novel circumstances, and then because he was enjoying it. The dignified old man had a benign effect upon him. It was as though he were sitting with a father to whom he could confess everything.

"The chicken is first-rate," the President opined.

"It really is," Archilochos conceded.

"And the champagne is also excellent."

"I never thought anything so good existed," Archilochos confessed.

"Let us chat as we eat; let's not shirk it. Let us talk about your lovely Chloé, who is your problem, who perplexes you," the old man proposed.

"I was terribly shocked today in the Héloïse Chapel," Archilochos said. "When I realized the truth for the first time."

"I rather had that impression," the President said.

"As I saw you sitting there," Arnolph confessed, "in the church, with all your decorations, it suddenly entered my mind that you had come to the wedding only because you and Chloé . . ."

"Had you had such a high opinion of me?" the old gentleman asked.

"You were my model. I thought you were a strict opponent of alcohol," Archilochos told him shyly.

"The newspapers cooked that up for me," the President growled. "The government is waging a campaign against alcoholism, so they always photograph me holding a glass of milk."

"It was also said that you are extremely austere in regard to morals."

"That's for the consumption of the Federation of Women's Clubs. Are you a teetotaler?"

"A vegetarian also."

"But now you're drinking champagne and eating chicken."

"I no longer have any ideals."

"I'm sorry to hear it."

"Everyone is a hypocrite."

"Including Chloé?"

"You know very well what Chloé is."

"The truth," the President remarked, laying aside a gnawed chicken bone and moving the candelabrum so that it no longer stood between them, "the truth is always rather embarrassing when it comes to light, not only in the case of women, but in the case of all human beings, and especially in the case of the government. Sometimes I too would like to rush out of my palace, which I consider monstrous from a purely architectural point of view, just as you rushed out of the Héloïse Chapel; but the way things are, I don't quite have the courage, and so I climb surreptitiously over the wall. I don't want to defend any of the persons involved, least of all myself. This is, in general, an area which is hard to discuss in a decent way, and if it can be done at all, then only at night between two people. Because views and moralities which don't belong are too apt to get mixed up in the matter, and because the virtues, passions, and defects of men lie so close together and contempt and hatred can easily arise where respect and love would be the only proper sentiments. I want to say only one thing to you, my dear good fellow: If there is one person in the world whom I envy, it is you, and if there is one person for whose future I am gravely alarmed, it is also you. . . . I had to share Chloé with many others," he said after a while, hunched in the Biedermeier chair, educating Archilochos with an almost tender note in his voice. "She was a queen in a dark, elemental kingdom. She was a courtesan. The most famous in the city. I do not want to make this out any better than it is; I am too old to do that. But I am grateful that she gave me her love, and I think back on no one in this world with greater gratitude. Now she has turned away from all of us and come to you. Therefore her day of rejoicing was for us a farewell and a thanksgiving."

The aged President fell silent. Dreamily, he ran his hand over his carefully groomed goatee. The valet poured champagne, and from outside they heard the staccato commands and goose-stepping of the body-guard. Archilochos, too, leaned back in his chair, musing with wonderment at the now utterly useless grenade in his coat pocket. Through the window curtain he spied Fahrcks's car waiting in front of the Economics Ministry.

"Now as for you, my dear, good fellow," the President continued softly after a while, lighting a small cigar which the valet had handed him (Archilochos, too, was smoking), "I understand your tempestuous feelings. What man in your situation would not be offended? But these altogether natural emotions are precisely those we should combat, for they can do the greatest harm. I cannot help you—who could do that? I can only hope that you will learn to ignore a fact which no one can deny, but which will become inconsequential if you have the strength to believe in the love that Chloé is offering you. The miracle which has happened between you two is only possible and only credible through the workings of love. Outside that love, it becomes a farce. Thus you must walk across a narrow bridge over dangerous abysses, as Mohammedans must tread the edge of a sword when they enter their paradise—I read something of the sort once upon a time. But do take a little more chicken," he urged the thwarted murderer. "It really is excellent, and there's always comfort to be found in good food."

Archilochos sat there, surrounded by the glow of candles, absorbing the delicious warmth of the room. On the walls, in heavy gold frames, hung earnest, long-since-deceased statesmen and heroes who had entered into eternity and regarded him thoughtfully, strangely, sublimely. A hitherto unknown peace had entered his soul, an incomprehensible serenity, evoked not only by the President's words—what did words amount to, after all?—but by his kindly, paternal, courteous manner.

"A grace has been conferred upon you," the old

statesman added. "There are two possibile reasons for this grace, and it depends upon you which of them is the valid one: love, if you believe in that love, or evil, if you do not believe in that love. Love is a miracle that is eternally possible; evil is a fact that is eternally present. Justice condemns evil, hope longs to reform it, and love overlooks it. Only love is capable of accepting grace as it is. There is nothing more difficult, I know. The world is terrible and meaningless. The hope of finding a meaning behind all the meaninglessness, behind all the terror, can be preserved only by those who nevertheless can love."

He fell silent, and for the first time Archilochos was again able to think of Chloé without a shudder, without horror.

Then,

when the candles had burned down, the President helped Archilochos into the coat with the now useless grenade in its pocket and accompanied him, since the elevator happened to be out of order down to the main entrance. Because, as he said, he did not want to bother Ludwig, who, stiff and impeccable, had fallen asleep standing beside his master's chair—a feat which, the old man declared, should certainly be respected. And so the two walked down through the deserted palace, down the broad, curving staircase, Archilochos consoled, content with the world, longing for Chloé, the President behaving rather like a museum curator, turning on the lights in this or that hall and making the necessary explanations. Here he received state visitors, he would remark, pointing into a lofty reception room; or here he accepted the resignation of the Premier, twice a month; and here in this intimate salon with its nearly genuine Raphael he had had tea with the Queen of England and her prince consort, and had nearly fallen asleep when the prince consort began talking about the navy; nothing bored him so much as naval stories, and only the quick-wittedness of the Chief of Protocol had averted a national disaster; the Chief of Protocol had awakened him at the crucial moment and whispered to him a properly naval reply. Otherwise, he must say, the two English visitors had been very nice.

Then they bade each other good-by, two friends who had had a full talk, who had made peace with one another. From the main entrance the old man once more waved, smiling, serene. Archilochos looked back. The palace loomed into the cold night, dark now, like a gigantic, over-ornamented chest of drawers. The quarter moon was no longer visible. He walked between the saluting bodyguards and reached the Quai de l'État, but then turned into Etter Lane between the Nuncio's residence and the Swiss Embassy, for he saw Fahrcks's car roaring toward him from the direction of the Economics Ministry. In front of Pfyffer's Bar on the Rue Stäbi he took a cab; he had no desire to meet Fahrcks again. Back home, he raced across the garden, obsessed by the single thought of taking Chloé into his arms. The rococo palace was brightly lit. Uproarious singing surged toward him. The front door was open. Dense yellow swaths of pipe and cigar smoke filled the air. Brother Bibi with his brood had now taken possession of the entire house. Everywhere, members of the gang were sitting and lying around, drunk, jabbering, on the sofas, under the tables, tangled in curtains that had been dragged from the windows. All the tramps, pimps, and fancy-boys of the city seemed to be assembled. In the beds women screeched, bare breasts gleamed; gallow birds sat in the kitchen, stuffing their bellies, smacking their lips, drinking up the liquor closets and the cellar. Matthew and Sebastian were playing hockey in the dining room with two wooden legs for sticks. In the hall Uncle Captain was practicing knife throwing with Mama dear, while Jean-Christophe and Jean-Daniel were playing marbles with his glass eye and Théophile and Gottlieb, sluts on their laps, were sliding down the banisters. Filled with an evil presentiment, Arnolph ran upstairs, past the art dealer Nadelör, who still lay delirious in his bed, through the boudoir, where a male chorus and the splash of water could be heard from the bathroom, along with Magda-Maria's shrill voice; when he rushed into the bedroom, Brother Bibi lay in bed with a mistress (undressed). Nowhere in the house had there been any sign of Chloé.

"Where is Chloé?"

"What's this, Brother," Bibi said reproachfully, puffing at a cigar. "Never enter a bedroom without knocking."

That was as far as Bibi got. His brother had undergone a metamorphosis. He had rushed into his palace filled with the tenderest emotions, full of love, full of longing for Chloé. Now all these emotions turned to wrath. The folly of having supported this family for years, the impudence with which they had taken over his house, the fear that he had lost Chloé through his own fault, transformed him into a raging lion. He became an Ares, a Greek god of war, as Passap had predicted. Picking up Passap's wire sculpture, he smashed it down upon his cigar-smoking brother sprawled out in the marital bed with his trull. With a cry, Brother Bibi leaped out of bed, received a right hook to the jaw, and staggered to the door, where Arnolph pounded him again, then turned to the trull, whom he dragged by the hair into the hall and hurled at the Captain, who, alarmed by Bibi's roars, had come racing forward, whereupon the two went bouncing down the stairs. From all the doors sharpers, pimps, and other scum came rushing at him, some members of his own family, like Théophile and Gottlieb, whom he sent flying down the winding staircase, together with Nadelör, Renaissance bed and all, then Sebastian and Matthew, whom he pounded to a pulp, then Magda-Maria with her lover (Chinese), whom he threw naked through the splintering panes of the window into the garden outside, then unknown creatures. Wooden legs whistled through the air, chair legs, blood spurted, whores fled, Mama dear fainted dead away, fancy boys and counterfeiters, shoulders hunched, whistling like rats in their terror, beat a quick retreat. Arnolph swung, choked, scratched, struck, smashed, pounded heads together, raped a mistress while wooden legs, brass knuckles, rubber truncheons, and bottles hailed down on him, rose again, freed himself, foaming at the mouth, used a round table as a shield, vases, chairs, oil paintings, Jean-Christophe, and Jean-Daniel as missiles, and steadily advancing, crushing all resistance, his clothes in tatters, cursing steadily, drove the whole scurvy band out of his house, in which the wallpaper now hung in shreds, waving banners in the icy drafts that swept out the billows of tobacco smoke. Finally, when they were all outside, he threw the hand grenade after the howling crew, and the explosion illuminated the garden along with the first light of morning.

Then he stood for a long time at the entrance of his demolished mansion, staring into the quickening dawn which rose silvery behind the elms and the firs of the garden. Warm gusts of wind lashed the trees, shook them. A thaw was beginning. The ice of the roof melted; water gurgled in the gutter. Everything dripped; huge banks of cloud swept over the roofs and gardens, heavy and fecund; rain sifted down in thin sheets. Bruised, half dressed, shivering, Nadelör limped past him into the damp morning.

"You as a Christian!"

Archilochos paid no attention to him. He stared into space out of swollen eyes, bloodstained, his wedding suit tattered, the lining of the jacket hanging out, his glasses lost.

He began searching for Chloé.

"Good Lord, Monsieur Arnolph!" Georgette cried when he appeared at the counter and demanded a Pernod. "Good Lord, what is the matter with you?"

"I can't find Chloé."

The restaurant was full of customers. Auguste was waiting on tables. Archilochos finished his Pernod and asked for another.

"Have you looked everywhere?" Madame Bieler asked.

"At Passap's, at the Bishop's, everywhere."

"She will turn up," Georgette encouraged him. "Women don't get lost so easily, and they're often just where you least expect them."

Then she poured him a third Pernod.

"At last," Auguste said with a sigh of relief to the cycling fans. "Now he's drinking."

Archilochos went on with his search. He forced his way into convents, boardinghouses, furnished apartments. Chloé could not be found. He wandered through his deserted palace, through the empty gardens, stood in the wet leaves. Nothing. The trees sighed, the clouds raced above the roofs. Suddenly homesickness overcame him, a longing for Greece, for red cliffs and dark groves, for the Peloponnesus.

Two hours later he embarked. As the *Julia,* siren wailing, wrapped in her own smoke, glided into the fog, a car filled with Fahrcks's activists came roaring up and fired a few bullets after the ship, meant for the deserting assassin; but they only slashed the wearily waving green and golden landing flag.

Mr. and Mrs. Weeman were on the *Julia,* and they regarded him anxiously when, one afternoon, he came up to them.

Mediterranean. The deck in sunlight. Deck chairs everywhere. Archilochos said: "I have had the honor of speaking with you several times."

"Well," Mr. Weeman rumbled.

Arnolph apologized. It had all been a misunderstanding, he said.

"Yes," Mr. Weeman agreed.

Then Archilochos asked permission to help with the excavations in his old homeland.

"Well," Mr. Weeman replied, folding the *Journal of Antiquities.* Then he said, while filling his stubby pipe: "Yes . . ."

And so Archilochos dug for antiquities in Greece, in a part of the Peloponnesus which did not in the least conform to the picture he had conceived of his land of origin. He shoveled under a merciless sun. Gravel, snakes, scorpions, and a few crippled olive trees against the horizon. Low, barren hills, dried-up springs, not even bushes. A vulture circled over his head, stubborn, refusing to be frightened off. He hacked for weeks with a pick at a hill, streaming sweat, slowly hollowing out the hill. At last he exposed some shabby walls filled with sand, sand that grew fiery hot in the sun, crept under his fingernails, inflamed his eyes. Mr. Weeman hoped they had uncovered a temple of Zeus, Mrs. Weeman thought it a sanctuary of Aphrodite. The altercations of the pair could be heard for miles. Their Greek helpers had long since quit work. Mosquitoes buzzed, flies covered Arnolph's face, crawled over his eyes. Dusk fell. In the distance a mule brayed, shrill and wailing. The night was cold. Archilochos lay in his tent beside the excavation site, Mr. and Mrs. Weeman in the hotel in the capital of the district, a miserable hole some seven miles away. Nocturnal birds and bats fluttered around the tent. In the distance an unknown animal howled, perhaps a wolf; then it was quiet again. He fell asleep. Toward morning he imagined he heard soft footsteps. He slept on. As soon as the sun, red and fierce above the senselessly barren hills, touched his tent, he got up. He staggered to his solitary place of work, by the walls. It was still cold. High above, the vulture was still circling. Inside the walls it was still almost entirely dark. His limbs ached. He set to work with the shovel. Before him lay an oblong heap of sand, glistening in the semidarkness; but after the first few cautious probes he felt resistance. Is it Zeus or the goddess of love? he wondered, curious as to which of the two archaeologists was right. He set to work with both hands, scuffed the sand away, and exposed Chloé.

Scarcely daring to breathe, he stared at his beloved.

"Chloé," he cried, "Chloé, what are you doing here?"

She opened her eyes, but remained lying in the sand.

"Very simple," she said. "I followed you. We had two tickets, you know."

Then they sat on the wall and looked out over the Greek land, at the low, barren hills with the tremendous sun above them, at the crippled olive trees in the distance, and at the white gleam of the capital of the district on the horizon.

"This is our native land," she said. "Yours and mine."

"Where were you?" he asked. "I searched the whole city for you."

"At Georgette's. In the apartment upstairs."

Two dots moved in the distance, approaching. Mr. and Mrs. Weeman.

Then she delivered her speech on love, somewhat as Diotima long ago to Socrates—though not so profound a one, of course, for as the child of a Greek businessman (to straighten out the matter of her origins) Chloé Saloniki was of a more robust and practical temper.

"You see," she said, while the wind played with her hair and the sun moved ponderously higher and higher in the sky and the English couple approached steadily closer on their mules, "now you know what I was; that has been cleared up between us. I was sick of my work, which is hard work, like any honest work. But it made me sad. I had a longing for love, for someone to care for; I wanted to be available not only for a man's pleasure, but also for his sorrows. And one morning when the fog wrapped my little palace, one wintry, dark morning, as it had been for weeks, I read in *Le Soir* that a Greek wanted a Greek wife. Then I made up my mind to love *that* Greek, him alone and no one else, no matter what happened, no matter what he was like. And so I came to you, that Sunday morning at ten, with the rose. I didn't mean to hide what I was. I came in my best clothes. As I wanted to accept you as you were, I meant you to accept me as I was, and when I saw you sitting at the table, bashful, awkward, with the steaming milk and cleaning your glasses, I fell in love with you. But since you thought I was still an innocent girl, since you showed so little knowledge of the world that you did not guess my profession, as Georgette and her husband guessed it, I didn't dare to destroy your illusion. I was afraid of losing you, and so only made everything worse. Your love became a thing of ridicule, and when you realized the truth in the Héloïse Chapel, your love was shattered along with your world. It was good that that happened. You could not love me without the truth, and only love is stronger than truth, which threatened to destroy us. The love you had in your blindness had to be destroyed for the sake of clear-eyed love, which is the only kind that counts."

But some time passed

before Chloé and Archilochos were able to return home. The government crashed. Fahrcks, the Order of the Kremlin under his double chin, took the rudder. The night sky flared red. Everywhere flags, everywhere choruses chanting: "Ami, go home." Everywhere banners, huge portraits of Lenin and of the Russian Premier, who had just barely escaped overthrow. But the Kremlin was far away, the dollar needed, personal power tempting. Fahrcks moved into the Western camp, had the Chief of the Secret Police (Petit-Paysan's secretary) strung up, and thereafter resided in the most dignified manner in the Presidential Palace on the Quai de l'État, protected like his predecessor by the same bodyguard with golden helmets and white plumes, his red hair carefully barbered, his mustache cropped. He relaxed the stringency of his regime, his ideology faded, and one fine Easter Sunday he attended services at St. Luke's Cathedral. The bourgeois order returned, and with it Chloé and Archilochos; but they could no longer feel at ease. However, they tried it for a while. They turned their little palace into a boardinghouse. Passap rented a room; he was no longer in favor (in artistic matters Fahrcks stuck by socialist realism). Maître Dutour moved in, he too in reduced circumstances. So did Hercule Wagner with his enormous wife, he too deposed; likewise the overthrown President, still courteous, serenely surveying the course of affairs; finally Petit-Paysan (the merger with the Rubber and Lubricating Oil Cartel had proved his ruin), doing light housework: a bankrupt crew. Only the Bishop was missing. He had gone over to the New Presbyterians of the Penultimate Christians. The boarders drank milk, Perrier on Sundays, lived quietly, spending the summers under the trees of the garden, dreamy, at peace with their undemanding world. Archilochos was deeply troubled. He went to see his brother, who lived in a suburb with Mama, Uncle Captain, and the dear little ones, running a small plant nursery—the beating Arnolph had given him had worked wonders. (Matthew passed his teacher's examination, Magda-Maria taught kindergarten, the others worked in factories or entered the Salvation Army.) But Arnolph did not stay long at his brother's. The sturdy, upstanding atmosphere, the pipe-smoking captain, and Mama knitting bored him, as did Bibi, who now regularly attended the Héloïse Chapel in his stead. Four times a week.

"You look pale, Monsieur Arnolph," said Georgette, as he once again stood at the counter before her (behind her, above the bottles of brandy and liqueurs, Fahrcks now hung in the carved picture frame). "Do you have troubles?"

She handed him a glass of Pernod.

"Everyone drinks milk," he growled. "The cycling fans and even your husband now."

"What can little guys like us do?" Auguste said, still in his yellow jersey, rubbing his gleaming legs. "The government has launched another anti-alcohol campaign. Besides, I'm an athlete, after all."

Then Archilochos observed Georgette opening a bottle of Perrier.

"She, too," he thought regretfully. And while he lay beside Chloé in the canopied bed, behind the red curtain, logs burning in the fireplace, he said: "It's really very pleasant in our little palace with these contented, aging boarders. I don't want to complain, but this virtuous world we live in strikes me as uncanny. It seems to me that I have converted the world and it has converted me, so that it comes down to the same thing in the end and everything has been in vain."

Chloé had sat up while he talked.

"All this time I've been thinking about our wall, back in our native land," she said. "That time I covered myself with sand to surprise you, and lay there that dark morning, looking up at the vulture circling above the field, I felt something hard underneath me, something stony, like two big round breasts."

"The goddess of love!" Archilochos cried, leaping out of bed. Chloé, too, got up.

"We must never stop seeking the goddess of love," she whispered. "Otherwise she will abandon us."

They dressed noiselessly, packed a suitcase, and when Sophie entered the bedroom at eleven o'clock next morning, after knocking in vain for a long time, she and the anxious boarders who pressed in after her found the room empty.

A NOTE ON THE TYPE

THE TEXT of this book was set on the Linotype in a face called *Times Roman,* designed by STANLEY MORISON for *The Times* (London), and first introduced by that newspaper in 1932.

Among typographers and designers of the twentieth century, Stanley Morison has been a strong forming influence, as typographical advisor to the English Monotype Corporation, as a director of two distinguished English publishing houses, and as a writer of sensibility, erudition, and keen practical sense.

Composed, printed, and bound by
The Haddon Craftsmen, Scranton, Pa.